UNLEASHED

ROSS SIBLINGS SERIES

Unleashed

Ross Siblings Series

Cherrie Lynn

Entangled Publishing, LLC
2614 South Timberline Road,
Suite 105
Fort Collins, CO 80525
Visit our website at www.entangledpublishing.com.

Select Contemporary is an imprint of Entangled Publishing, LLC.

Edited by Linda Ingmanson
Cover design by Fiona Jayde
Cover art from iStock

Manufactured in the United States of America

First Edition April 2009
Re-release July 2017

For Brandon, my husband and best friend.

Chapter One

"Aloha, gorgeous. How'd you like to run away with me to Hawaii?"

Kelsey Peterson had been taking a sip of her latte after she answered the phone ringing on her desk. The proposition that met her greeting—deep, breathy, undeniably male—sent the portion of the gulp she hadn't choked on spewing across her monitor. What the hell?

Hacking like a lifetime smoker, she gasped for oxygen and reached across her desk for tissues, mind still reeling. The instant he broke into laughter over the line, the world righted itself...somewhat. Still, it took a moment before she could form words, and he—damn him—seemed to be having the time of his life.

"I'm sorry," she said, "the receptionist told me Evan Ross was calling. Obviously, whoever you are, you've kidnapped him and taken over his body."

"Sounds kinky." The response was jovial, normal—the

Evan she'd known since college. So what if she'd enjoyed the fantasy for one nanosecond? "How are things on the dark side?" he asked. "Haven't made a decision to join us good guys yet?"

"You know we have to maintain our balance between good and evil." She began to mop up the mess she'd made as he chuckled. As a prosecutor in the district attorney's office, Evan agonized over her position as legal assistant to a defense attorney he often faced in court.

"How have you been, Kels?" Evan asked.

"Great!"

"Liar."

"Yeah, so? How are you?" That question was far more loaded than it sounded. For both of them.

"I'm actually good. I'm really, really good." Oh, God help her, his voice had taken on that sexy purr again. She strangled over the remaining latte caught in her windpipe and held the receiver away from her mouth while she tried to clear it. So much for playing it cool. She hadn't spoken to Evan in weeks and, at this rate, it might be a few more before she was able.

She could hear him going on, oblivious to her struggles, and she brought the phone back to her ear. "It just so happens I've been struck by inspiration," he was saying.

"Really," she wheezed.

Concern suddenly tinged his voice. "Hey, are you all right? I didn't mean to freak you out back there. Man, this is going over well."

"Sorry, just—" She took another quick sip. "Okay. I'm a dweeb. So what is this you're rattling on about?"

"The very thing that made you nearly hack up a lung. I'm taking you to Hawaii. For a week. All expenses paid. Notice it was a statement and not a question?"

"You're…taking me…what?"

"It seems I'm stuck with a useless paid-for honeymoon. It

was a gift from my parents."

"I didn't know about that."

He cleared his throat. "Well, I never bothered to cancel the reservations and, as it turns out, the plane tickets are nonrefundable. We'll lose Courtney's either way, but I happen to be staring at the airline website right now, ready to jump on a ticket for you on the same flight. Just say the word."

"I'm sure you have two dozen other buddies who would be thrilled to take this trip with you. Why me?"

"They probably snore and don't smell nearly as good as you."

"Jesus Christ, Evan Ross."

He burst out laughing. "I think you say that at some point every time we talk."

Kelsey tapped her pen against her keyboard, smiling absently. She loved hearing from Evan, always had. Since her divorce from his former best friend, Todd, there hadn't been very many opportunities to talk to him. Everything had changed last winter. She couldn't speak to Evan now without remembering one conversation in particular. It had been very brief, but it had involved her screaming at him like a banshee, crying and cursing into her cell phone, while he maintained dead silence on the other end. God, what a nightmare. She eased her head down on her desk, cringing as she always did whenever she thought about it.

"Come on. I know you want it. I know you need to get away. We both do."

Oh, she wanted it all right. And she didn't mean the trip. Well, maybe the trip. "Yes, but um…together? If my boss found out, he wouldn't be pleased. Consorting with the enemy and all that."

"Of course. It's a covert op. No problem."

"Evan… I can't afford to pay you for my ticket." It hurt to say it, but there it was.

"That's not even an issue. Don't give it another thought, and I mean that."

"Do your parents know, then?"

"Yeah, but you don't have to worry, they're discreet old souls. We have their blessing. So bring on the next objection, and let me slap that one down, too."

She doodled with absent ferocity. Hawaii. Hawaii! She'd never been. Evan had. If she was ever going to go, who better to go with? Why wouldn't her damn mind just shut up and let her accept? "I just can't."

"That's the easiest one of all. You can."

Kelsey's eyes widened as another thought occurred to her, and she glanced down at her desk calendar to be sure. "Wait a minute…wasn't your wedding supposed to be in two weeks?"

"Yep."

"And your honeymoon to start right after?"

He chuckled. "Yep. So you see, I need an answer. Like now, Kelsey. Now."

"There's no way, then. Work—"

"I'll have a big case waiting for me against your esteemed employer just as soon as I get back, so don't talk to me about work. Hit me again."

"I'm going to ask you one more time. Why me? Is it pity? Because I don't need that—"

"God, no. Nothing like that." He was quiet for a moment, and she lifted her head to watch the quote on her screensaver marquee scroll by. Without the bitter, the sweet ain't as sweet. It was from Vanilla Sky. Evan went on, his voice somber now. "You and me, we've been through too much together for pity to play into it. We've been friends forever. What's wrong with two friends getting away from it all?"

When the friends are male and female, she thought. When they're apparently sharing a room…and a bed…

in a honeymoon suite? When her occupation was all about causing his defeat. And when they had such a screwy history. Ten years certainly wasn't forever, though it sometimes felt like it.

Evan being sin incarnate had something to do with the wrongness of it, as well. His voice alone, rich and melodic over the line, had her wanting to slide her skirt up her thighs and plunge her hand into her panties right there in her office. One more word in that deep, erotic tone he'd used before and she might not be able to resist the urge.

She could just imagine what he looked like right now—his black hair perpetually tousled, his sharp green eyes fringed with eyelashes that could make a cover girl weep with envy. Eyebrows two decisive black brushstrokes. Probably had his jacket off and his tie loosened and his white shirtsleeves rolled up over his olive-skinned forearms, as always when he was on the job but not at court or in a meeting. As if he couldn't bear the restraint a minute longer than necessary. He might even be kicked back in his chair, his feet propped on his desk...

Her boss, Jack Ballinger, always said when he tried a case against Evan, the jury's reaction to his opposing counsel concerned him more than their reaction to the defendant. More specifically, the women's reaction. "One twinkle from that boy's eye and they're ready to throw their goddamned panties at him during closing arguments," she'd overheard Jack say. Kelsey thought it was pretty damned misogynistic of him, but that was Jack.

She fidgeted in her seat, not wanting to prove her boss right just from a simple phone call from the man himself. Yes, she and Evan had been friends for years, but she'd had a raging crush on him long before she'd met and married his best friend. It had subsided...somewhat. From a roaring flame to gently smoldering embers. But now that she was single—and so was Evan—she hadn't been able to stop it from flaring to life once again.

Did thirty-year-olds even have crushes?

Oh, this could not happen. There was no way. The idea seemed like pure bliss, but the reality, she knew, would be a nightmare. Another one, and she didn't think their friendship could bear that kind of strain now. He didn't know what he was doing.

"Evan, I think this is the sweetest thing anyone has ever offered me. But I can't."

He groaned playfully. "Please don't leave me like this, with my vision of having you isolated and helpless in Waikiki so cruelly denied."

She couldn't help but laugh. It was all innuendo on his part, at least she knew that much. Impossible flirt.

A week with that kind of innuendo might prove to be her undoing.

Her phone emitted a muffled ring and, upon checking the display, it was her turn to groan, though there was nothing playful about it. Jack. "Hey, I really have to go—"

"Not until you at least give me a maybe."

"Oh, you—"

"Give me an answer or I'm going to call Jack myself and request your time off."

"No!"

"The reason I'm asking you is that no one else I know deserves this as much as you do. And we haven't hung out in a while. I feel bad about that. Let me make it right. Come on."

Maybe it was time for her to come undone.

"Evan?" She lowered her voice to a throaty phone-sex pitch.

"Yes, yes?"

"I'll think about it." Grinning like a fiend, she hit the button that disconnected him then put on her best professional voice to greet her boss on the other line.

Lisa Scott's blue eyes were bright and ravenous as Kelsey finished filling her in on the strange conversation that had taken place that morning. "Evan Ross, whose pants you've wanted to get into since college, has invited you to Hawaii? Both of you now free and unattached—and your problem is what, exactly?"

Kelsey sighed as she stirred sweetener into her iced tea, sweeping a glance around their favorite diner. It was hopping with the usual lunchtime crowd. Sometimes—rarely, though—she saw Evan in here. "I think you just summed it up."

"Damn, girl. Please tell me you're not still in the all-men-are-pigs stage. Because it's just not true."

"It's not that. I know Evan's a good guy. Can't seem to sustain a relationship, though. And except with Courtney, he's usually been the one to cut and run."

"Uh-huh." Lisa smoothed a hand over her very pregnant belly. They'd had to pull the table closer to Kelsey so Lisa could squeeze into the booth, the only available seating. It had been hilarious to witness. "I'm waiting."

Kelsey shrugged, picking through her barely touched Caesar salad. "What? I caught his fiancée screwing my husband. You know this. I didn't hesitate to call Evan and scream into his ear about it. I didn't handle the situation well. It's a miracle he still speaks to me at all."

"But he does. He invited you on vacation with him. It sounds like the man is eternally grateful. He knows you probably saved him from a very expensive divorce on down the road."

"Maybe."

"And I thought you handled the situation exceptionally well, given that I'd have plucked every blonde hair from Courtney's head, if I'd caught her with Daniel." Lisa leaned

forward—as much as she was able—and placed her hand over
Kelsey's on the tabletop. "Please go. I promise you, it'll be all
right. Could be just what you both need. He wouldn't have
invited you if he held anything against you. Or if he didn't
care."

"I know he cares. But the way I see it, there's only a
couple of possible outcomes here. One: nothing will change,
and it really is two friends just getting away together, though
I'm sure I'll fall hard for him again. Two: we'll have a week of
wild sex during which I'll fall even harder and end up getting
my heart broken. Neither one is very appealing right now."

"Three: you have a week of wild sex and live happily
ever after. Or four: you get him out of your system and you're
totally free from the burden, end of story. Or! Five: you meet
the man of your dreams in Hawaii, and send Evan home to
tell us you're never coming back."

"It's far more likely that he'll find a girl and send me back
alone. I didn't even think of that. Thanks a lot."

"Shut up. You don't have to buy a pair of shoes just
because you tried them on. They may look great sitting on
the shelf, but that doesn't mean they won't feel like medieval
torture devices on your feet once you wear them around for a
few days. It's the same thing with men."

"I know me, though. If I sleep with him, I'm done for."

"You think too much. And you'd really better go to
Hawaii or I'm giving up on you. Your divorce is final. You
look great. You're ripe, girl, and we'll go shopping for a new
bikini, and you'll look gorgeous in it and I'll hate your guts.
Don't you dare hesitate to let him take it off you, should he
feel so inclined. You're over He Who Shall No Longer Be
Named and you're ready to have fun. Right?"

"Yeah, I'm over it. Not sure about the fun part."

"Sweetie, you had such a long, cold winter, but it's over.
It's summer. You'll never have a better opportunity to get half

naked around Evan Ross." Lisa lowered her voice and leaned farther across the table. "Come on, Kelsey. You know as well as I do that your vibrator can only do so much until you start craving a warm body to hang on to again."

For the second time that day, Kelsey nearly spit out her drink. "Yeah, well I don't even own one of those."

"Now I know what to get you for your birthday. Unless Evan removes all need for one between now and then. I demand that you go and get laid. Get drunk and have sensational toe-curling sex on the beach while I freaking sit at home and gestate."

Kelsey barked with laughter. "You're crazy. I'd rather sit at home gestating with a wonderful husband than go through this turmoil. You don't know how lucky you are."

Lisa sat back, an utterly satisfied smile on her face. She patted her swelling belly again. Her friend was the most adorable pregnant woman Kelsey had ever seen. She had such fun with it. "Well, you're not behaving in a manner conducive to landing a husband, woman. You generally have to leave your house for that. Evan is certainly a keeper. Maybe someday…"

"Oh, okay, he's invited me on one trip, he hasn't proposed."

"Yet."

"Lisa!"

Too late; the girl was having way too much fun. Whenever Lisa laughed now, her belly bounced in a way that only made her giggle harder. And Kelsey's earlier words had rung as true as any she'd ever spoken. Lisa had a fantastic marriage, a beautiful family. It was all Kelsey had ever wanted, and the very thing she'd been denied on a cold, dreary day six months ago—only a week before Christmas. Her world had crumbled during an ill-timed trip home from work for some Advil.

It was heavy on her mind as she drove back to the office. Evan's phone call had brought it all crashing back. For months she'd considered it a stroke of fate that she'd been lost in her thoughts that day and driven right past the drugstore, her intended destination. Instead of turning around, she'd decided it would be easier to continue on the few extra blocks to her house. Maybe she could even lie down for fifteen minutes or so to see if her head would quit its dull, nagging ache. Looking back she wondered if that damn headache had been an omen.

Todd's car parked in their driveway in the middle of the day had been an odd sight, but she didn't think anything of it…until she heard their muffled cries when she entered her front door. She staggered to her bedroom in a blind rage to find her husband lying beneath his best friend's fiancée in Kelsey's own bed.

She couldn't remember much after that. She just knew it had been ugly. Evan came to get the scandalized girl after Kelsey's hysterical and utterly embarrassing phone call, since Todd's car keys—both sets—had mysteriously wound up at the bottom of the swimming pool when he tried to leave with Courtney.

The look on Evan's face when he got there, the raw fury and devastated betrayal, was etched into her memory and would remain there from now on. Even in the throes of her own anger, she'd wanted to comfort him, but from the moment she saw him she knew he was beyond it. She and Courtney had been too busy calling an unspoken truce long enough to pull him and Todd apart in the front yard.

Kelsey would have been more than happy to let them go at it, because Evan had been so furious he'd have given Todd exactly what he deserved. But Todd clearly wasn't worth Evan getting slapped with an assault charge and jeopardizing the career he'd worked so hard to attain. Evan had refused to leave Kelsey alone with Todd until she had some backup. Lisa and Daniel had come to her rescue in that regard. She'd nearly collapsed in relief when they showed up and Evan hustled a mouthing, cursing Courtney to his truck, depositing her in the passenger seat. She would never forget the last searing glance he'd thrown her before he got in and drove away. She didn't know to this day what she'd read in that gaze.

Lisa and Daniel—God bless them—had finally taken her home with them, where she was left to stare helplessly at the broken, irreparable pieces of her marriage, her life. The moment she'd slammed open the bedroom door to see Todd and Courtney in all their naked glory...that moment had been the end, but more for her husband than for her. In the days that followed, he'd told her he was sorry it came to this, that he knew he should have done the right thing, but he wasn't happy anymore. Life was too short. Simple as that.

And she'd been dismissed.

She couldn't fool herself; she'd seen his unhappiness. He'd rejected all her suggestions to make it better, and finally she'd given up, hoping it would work itself out.

Not a good choice, obviously.

Chapter Two

"It's just one week, Lisa. I don't need to pack my entire closet."

"Hey, you never know when you might need this stuff."

"They have stores in Honolulu. I'm almost certain of it."

Lisa giggled and pulled yet another strappy top from Kelsey's closet. "See? He'll want to eat you alive in this. God, to have your figure. Of course, I shouldn't complain. I keep deliberately wrecking mine." She patted her tummy. Kelsey had spent all day last weekend helping her arrange the nursery while Daniel was away on business, and now Lisa was returning the favor by helping Kelsey pack for her trip and giving commentary on every item in her suitcase.

"I'm going to ban you from the closet. Get away." Kelsey laughed, pulling the shirt away and sticking it back in. "We're done, I have more than enough. I don't want to give him a hernia if he tries to lift my bags."

Lisa continued her perusal of Kelsey's clothes, shoes and purses. "Oh, he looks capable enough. You did pack condoms, right?"

"No way."

Lisa whirled on her. "Are you freaking insane?"

"If he happens to see them in my bag, what will he think?"

"That he's about to get laid! Or you are, with or without him."

Kelsey erupted into a fit of giggles, her heart slamming in her chest at the thought. Her fingers clenched hard on the pink legal pad she held, the one with her packing list…and a dozen other lists that pertained to more mundane, less panic-inducing things. During the two weeks since she'd given in and accepted Evan's offer she'd felt like a schoolgirl nursing her first crush. It wasn't healthy to feel this way, not about him.

Lisa was going on. "Say you're both thinking along that line. Then you unconsciously grope for one another in the middle of the night and you're a hot inch away from doing the nasty and suddenly it hits you that you have no protection. That sucks, Kelsey. How do you think I ended up like this for the third freaking time?"

She decided it best not to inform her friend that in that scenario, nary a responsible thought would cross her mind. "We're both clean and I'm on the pill. We got checked out after our significant others decided they liked one another better than they liked us. We talked about it."

"Okay, well if you trust him…but where's he been since? Didn't you say he was a bit of a player?"

"He was never a player. He was more like a serial monogamist. But it's not like any of this is going to matter. If there's anything I know, it's my relationship with Evan. He thinks of me as his kid sister or something. Even though we're the same age."

"After everything you've told me I can't believe you two never got in on in college. How did you fall so fast into the friend trap?"

"We met when we were partnered on a project in one of our classes and hit it off. I fell madly in love but he had a girlfriend. Then summer break happened. We came back in the fall and he had a different girlfriend. And so on and so forth until I met Todd. We had the worst timing imaginable. Not that it mattered. He was never interested in me like that."

"Did he tell you that?"

"Well, no. Because we never talked about these things, because I'm like his kid sister. Remember?"

"Don't let this hurt your feelings, Kels, but you thought you knew everything about that whoring bastard you married, too. You're going to be immersed in this tropical, romantic atmosphere with Evan and it's going to happen. Mark my words."

Kelsey chewed the tip of the pen she'd been using to check off list items. Lisa's first words had cut her; she couldn't deny it. She also couldn't deny the truth in them. "I almost want to prove you wrong, just to be a bitch."

Lisa laughed. "We need a code word. Because if—no, when—something goes down, I just want to know I was right. That way I can still get the goods even if other people are hovering."

"Whatever. What's the code?"

"Hmm. How about waves."

"Waves?"

"Yeah, I'll just ask you how the waves are. The enthusiasm of your answer will tell me all a best friend needs to know."

"What if I don't kiss and tell?"

Lisa only barked with laughter, choosing not to dignify that with a response. "What did your mom say when you finally told her what you were doing?"

Kelsey took on her mom's screech. "'Kelsey Ann! Wasn't he the best man at your wedding!' You'd think I was planning a bank heist."

"Oooh, scandal! I love it!" Lisa froze for a moment, then grabbed Kelsey's hand to place on her stomach. "Feel this.

She's turning cartwheels."

Kelsey smiled at the sensation pushing insistently under her palm. Emotion welled up in her, not just from her own maternal longings—God, she would probably never get to have kids—but for Lisa and her family, who had been her rock over these past several months. Lisa was the only person Kelsey talked to every day. Most of the friends she'd made here had been Todd's friends and had followed him after their split. All except for Evan.

Her heart warmed at the thought of him. And then turned so cold it burned. He wasn't hers, never had been, probably never would be, no matter how many Hawaiian vacations they took together.

She pulled her hand away and impulsively hugged her friend. It was heartfelt, but also an attempt to hide a sudden glimmer of tears. "That's awesome. I'm so happy for you guys."

"You'll get your turn, chick. I know it. You deserve it too much."

Kelsey blinked away the wetness and pulled back, promptly turning to walk over to her bed where her suitcase lay open. "Well, I only hope you can hold on for a week until I get home. I'd love to be there. You'd better call me, even if I'm still in Hawaii."

"You know it."

Lisa left soon after, and she took all pretenses of Kelsey's good humor with her. Deflated, she turned on her TV for company and began feverishly cleaning her already spotless apartment. There wasn't much of it to clean. She didn't want to think, didn't want to consider what she might have gotten herself into by accepting Evan's offer. As she'd told Lisa, there couldn't be a good outcome either way it went.

She straightened the bedcovers she would just mess up again in a couple of hours, dusted her knickknacks, surveyed

her closet and contemplated which outfits she could spare to
the women's shelter. There certainly were people in the world
suffering far worse situations than she, and helping them in
any way never failed to lift her spirits when she was down.
Maybe she could go volunteer for a while tomorrow. She
desperately needed that lift now, and she needed something
to occupy her time on the last full day before she and Evan
jetted off.

But her mad housecleaning and good-doing could only
keep the thoughts and memories at bay for so long. Once
unleashed, they consumed her.

The past couple of weeks had been hard. Feelings she'd
managed to bury since Todd's betrayal had weighed heavy
on her since she and Evan had begun to talk more. He often
called to check on her, make sure she was managing, see if
there was anything she needed. She'd seen him around the
courthouse a couple of times while she was filing papers and
running errands, and her heart had dropped to the pit of her
stomach every time. But those had only been brief, rushed
encounters. Despite the pain of it, she wanted to see him,
needed to see him. And she had a whole week of him ahead
of her. She should be happy. If nothing else, she was getting
an opportunity to spend time alone with one of her favorite
people in the world.

God, to be so conflicted.

She couldn't imagine how anyone who knew Evan well
could betray him like Todd and Courtney had. Soulless, they
were simply soulless. It was the only explanation. Surveying
her wardrobe, she absently jerked out the blue blouse she'd
been wearing the day she caught them—pathetic that she still
remembered what she was wearing—because it had to go.
She stuffed it deep into her sack of donations.

Evan inviting her on this trip was just like him, and if she
hadn't accepted, he would have offered it to someone else and

expected nothing in return. He came from money—his father owned half their mid-sized Texas town and his mother was like some freaking Italian goddess, but there was no spoiled rich-boy trip with him. Even after the events of last Christmas, he was still upbeat. Still Evan. She didn't know who the hell she was anymore.

But the last time she'd seen him before his call two weeks ago had been at her divorce hearing, just one of many events of the past few months that made her want to crawl under a rock and never emerge again. Evan had been in the courtroom for plea bargain hearings. Upon first seeing him as she entered the room, she'd wanted to turn on her heel and flee, wondering simultaneously how she could possibly face him today of all days and how in the hell it was possible for a man to look as comfortable and at ease in a suit as he did in jeans and a T-shirt. But she couldn't leave and there was no place to hide. Without hesitation he'd come over to hug her, and he'd sat with her when he wasn't dealing with other attorneys or standing at the bench.

When lunchtime rolled around and they still hadn't reached her case on the clogged-up docket, he'd insisted on taking her out to lunch, though the thought of food had wrenched her gut. She'd fought tears the entire time: riding with him, sitting in the restaurant, watching his every little move with fascination. Somehow, she'd managed to hold it together. She'd even managed to eat at his prodding.

Seeing him that day had given her strength and torn her apart all at once. She'd been mourning the demise of her marriage, but watching him work—admiring both his ruthlessness with the defense lawyers and his compassion for any victims who were present—had filled her with a heartache so intense not all her tears that day were for Todd. She'd shed a few for what might have been, if she'd only opened her mouth so long ago and told Evan how she felt. If it would have even mattered.

After the judge declared her divorced from Todd later that afternoon and the hearing was closed, she'd ambled back to where Evan sat watching with a tightness to his jaw she'd seen only when he was furious and holding it in. He'd wiped it away as she wordlessly plopped down next to him. And without comment, he'd picked up her hand, turned it over and drawn a little smiley face on her palm with his pen. The gesture had her blinking back tears as she looked up at him, and he'd smiled and kissed her forehead before standing to head back to his office. He'd stayed later than he needed to, just to be there for her.

She'd left that smiley face on her hand until it faded. Should have gotten the thing tattooed on for all the comfort it gave her. Even now she could still feel his fingers holding her hand, the tickle of the pen tip on her flesh.

And that was how Evan had always been. Encouraging her, telling her everything was going to be all right. Any time she'd found herself in a jam back in school, he was there to bail her out, whether it was dropping everything to help her with a paper or escorting a drunken, pawing frat brother away from her at a party.

To hell with it. Kelsey left the depths of her closet and made a beeline for the phone in the kitchen, sending her two cats fleeing in the process. Her fingers tapped out his cell number from memory and her breath froze up in her lungs in anticipation as it began to ring. When she heard it being answered, she nearly choked, and then the sound of his voice sent a shiver down to her toes. It made a stop in several other places along the way.

"Hey, you."

Oh, God, yes, sin incarnate. Was she pathetic because it gave her a warm glow that he had her number in his contacts? She struggled to sound casual and cheery. "Hi! What are you up to?"

"Not much. Just got home. I'm outside feeding my dogs—" His voice became distant suddenly, as if he'd pulled the phone away from his ear. "Dammit, get off me, you big bastard!"

Laughing, she imagined the scene that was playing out right now. She'd seen it before. Evan had Great Danes. They got so excited when he fed them they nearly took him down every time, and being that they were the size of small horses, sometimes they succeeded. "Are those my babies Zeus and Hera?" she asked.

"Babies, yeah. Ponies, maybe. You want them?"

As usual, he had a way of putting her at ease. Banter she could handle. True feelings—yeah, not so much. "I'm sure my landlord and my cats will love me for that. Dogs bigger than my apartment."

He chuckled. "I swear one of these days they're going to knock me down and eat me alive."

"You shouldn't starve them so much," she teased.

"Damn dogs eat more than I do. Hang on just a sec, Kelsey."

There was a rustling as if he was putting the phone in his pocket, and she had a few moments to ponder the imagery of him being knocked down and eaten alive by her. She could hear doggy grunts and whines and Evan scolding and laughing as he poured what sounded like an entire bag of dog food into their bowls. Then happy smacking sounds abounded.

"Okay, I'm back, dogs nourished. How are you?"

"Fine."

"Are you sure?"

Was she such an open book? The worst of it was that he knew her well enough that she couldn't lie to him. It was all those nights back in college—venting to each other about classes, professors and Evan's various girlfriends until the sun came up—that had given him this keen insight into her soul. Some of the best times of her life, even if he'd never laid a hand on her. "Yeah, just packing, nothing new," she said. "I just…" Wanted to hear your voice. "I wanted to see what you were up to. Are you excited?"

He scoffed. "You know I am." She heard a sound like a door opening and closing. He must have entered his house. "I'm all packed and ready myself. That's a record for me. I'm usually still throwing stuff in as I head out the door."

"I'm impressed, then."

"You should be." She could hear the smile in his voice and couldn't resist answering it with one of her own.

"You're doing the right thing, you know," he said.

The statement hit just a little too close to home. "Why do you say that?"

"Because a couple of times I've got the feeling you think you're not. We're going to have a great time, all right?"

"I know that. I'm looking forward to it."

"Good. So what are you doing right now?"

"Umm…sitting with my hair all in curlers, a green mud mask cracking on my face. It's not a pretty sight." An elaborate lie had always been their code for "nothing".

"Do you want to bring your curlers and mud mask to my house? I can throw a couple of steaks on the grill. We can celebrate our impending departure."

"Oh…" Momentarily, she lost her breath again. She hadn't expected this, though she'd been to his house many, many times. Only her husband had always been with her, and those two had been grilling the steaks while Kelsey and Courtney tried to find something in common to talk about. They'd always been like two different species, even back in their friendly days.

"It's kind of late for you to go to all that trouble—"

"It's only eight thirty. It's Friday night."

She'd wanted to see him and here was her opportunity. Why was she balking? If she was about to spend a week alone with the man, she needed to get herself re-accustomed to being around him. A lot. The last thing she wanted on her vacation was any awkwardness between them. Sharing a room…sharing a bed?

She ran wet and hot between her legs just thinking about it, and about the possibility of seeing him tonight. Only it would surely end in frustration for her, as it always had. It wasn't like they'd never shared a bed. She'd never had hang-ups about her looks, but she'd decided long ago—nine, ten years ago—that he must find her repulsive in some way, and she'd just never had it in her to seduce him. She hadn't even known where to start.

Regardless of whether she and Evan would ever take it to the next level, and even knowing the sight of his beautiful face would only break her heart, she was achingly lonely since Lisa had left. She needed company. His.

The contents of her checking account flashed before her mind, and she considered it before making her offer. "All right. Do you need me to bring anything from the store?"

"I'm pretty sure I have everything. If I don't, we'll just go after you get here." That smile was back in his voice. "I'm glad you're coming out. How long will you be?"

"Thirty, forty-five minutes?" She needed to shower and change. And wear sexy underwear, just in case. God, it was just like college on automatic replay, when she'd woken up every morning and wondered if today might be the day he came to his senses and realized they were meant to be together. Did she really want to put herself through that pathetic yearning again?

"Great. I'll see you then." The warmth in his tone curled up and settled around her heart, completely separate from the warmth curling in other places. As they hung up she could visualize his bedroom in her mind — she'd been in it only once a couple of years ago, shortly after he bought the house — with its deep jewel tones and the stately California king sleigh bed. She loved that bed. She could see them together in that bed.

Stop. Kelsey supposed she would never get it through her thick head that it wouldn't happen for them. Lisa was wrong. Evan could have any woman he wanted and he'd never wanted her. Kelsey had to face that fact, and accept that she would go to his house, eat and drink and laugh all night, then leave. They would go to Hawaii and do much of the same. And she would come home always having a friend in him, but never a lover.

She could accept it, but it wouldn't stop the hurt.

Chapter Three

Evan put the phone down on the kitchen counter, his smile still lingering even after her voice was gone. And that silly grin wouldn't seem to go away as he walked over to wash his hands in the sink and take two porterhouse steaks out of the freezer.

"Who's coming over?" his brother Brian yelled from the living room. He'd been earjacking again, despite the metalcore videos blaring from the TV.

"Kelsey. So get your slacker ass off my couch," Evan called back. The casual bystander would have detected a hint of hostility in his tone. They might have been right. Brian took it all in good humor, though at twenty-six he really did spend more time on Evan's and his parents' couches than anywhere else except the local tattoo parlor, where he was an artist. And a damn good one, at that, but he couldn't even commit fully to the things he excelled at and enjoyed.

"I knew you were talking to a girl. I can always tell." Brian padded into the kitchen, his feet bare and his long black and blue hair mussed, to get a Red Bull from the refrigerator. Dragons and flames and God only knew what else crawled down the skin of his arms from under the Nine Inch Nails T-shirt he wore. To look at him, one would think he was a pierced, tattooed nightmare, and it was true Evan often worried when Brian showed up unannounced that he might be harboring a fugitive. He was the reason Evan would probably never make a run for district attorney. But he was mostly harmless.

"Brian, piss off."

"So she's coming over because..."

"Because I invited her." Evan set the microwave to defrost and put in one steak. He turned to his pantry and collected the spices he needed for seasoning. "You do remember that we leave the day after tomorrow, right? And that I'm letting you stay here unsupervised the whole week? Don't make me regret it before I even leave."

"Whatever. So are you making a play for this girl?"

It was the burning question. Was he? She'd always been an enigma to him in college, and ten years later, she still was to an extent. Back then she'd been a strange mix. At a party she was the one laughing the loudest in the room, talking to the most people, staying till the wee hours. She might do that one night and close down the library the next, careful not to jeopardize her near-perfect GPA. He'd never known anyone more loyal, more genuinely nice. She was everyone's sweetheart. He'd been head over heels for her because of that alone.

But on the flip side, she'd been a bit prudish. She was only laughing the loudest until dirty jokes or sex talk started to fly, then she turned blood red and usually vanished. She'd never dated anyone that he knew of until she met Todd. Even now, just two days ago, she'd choked up when he got a little suggestive over the phone.

And by the time long ago when he'd decided that facet

of her personality didn't matter to him anymore, it was too late. Now there was another chance, but damn if there weren't even more problems.

He'd seen how her heartbreak of six months ago had wounded her down to the bone. He couldn't relate. Courtney's betrayal had delivered a swift sucker punch to his ego that over time morphed into relief. Most days he didn't waste a single thought on what the girl had done to him, and if he did, it was because he was thinking of Kelsey, and wishing he hadn't introduced two such destructive people into her life. She'd probably be better off right now if she'd never met him.

"We're just friends. I invited her because she's had a rough time these past few months and she deserves to have a little fun."

"And the fact that you always wanted to nail her has no bearing on it at all."

Evan whipped his head around. "What?"

Brian took a swig of his drink without taking his too-knowing gaze from Evan's. He smoothed a hand down over his black goatee. "I know you, man. Hey, it's cool. She's fun."

"Yeah."

"Dude, if you try to get through a week alone with her without getting a piece, I'd hate to be you. You'll come home with your nuts on ice. And I'll laugh."

"She really doesn't need one of her best friends putting the moves on her after what she's been through."

"What if she goes crazy and *begs* you for it, man? That happens to me all the time."

Ha. Not likely, not with Kelsey. Evan cast his brother a wry glance. "Right. How drunk did you have to get these girls?"

"Avoid the issue at hand. That's all right." Brian laughed in merry triumph and wandered off to the guest room he often crashed in. The rumbling thunder of Pantera's "Psycho

Holiday" began shaking the foundations of the house soon after. Evan sighed. He didn't mind heavy metal and went to concerts with his brother sometimes, though he usually felt wretched standing in plain sight of the dozen or so prosecutable offenses going on in the crowd around him. But Brian played his music at a volume that made Evan thankful he didn't have any close neighbors. Still, it didn't drown out the trill of his ringing cell phone. When he checked the display, he almost wished it had.

Etiquette didn't dictate that it was necessary to answer an ex-fiancée's call, especially when said ex-fiancée was with someone else. It wasn't like they had kids to discuss, or any reason at all to continue speaking to each other. More than anything else, Courtney had become a source of entertainment and information over the past several months. He almost let her call go to voicemail, but decided it probably best to deal with her and get it over with. If he didn't, she might call his mom, cry to her and get her all upset. The two had been great friends.

He answered with a curt, "Hey."

Her reply was soft and sad, as it usually was lately. The woman was miserable. But she'd made her bed. "Hey. What are you doing?"

You remember the girl whose marriage you wrecked? Yeah, I'm hanging out with her tonight.

It might not be the nicest reply. Sometimes he thought he was too nice. "Getting ready for company."

"It sounds like you're having a party."

"No, Brian's here. You know how he is."

"Oh. Never mind, then. I was hoping maybe we could talk tonight."

"Is Todd not in a talking mood tonight?"

There was a pause. "I left him."

Evan nearly dropped the phone. After he managed to

hang onto it, he gripped it with both hands and wrung it as if it were a neck. Hers. Casting an aimless *Why me?* to the ceiling, he brought it back to his ear.

"Sorry to hear."

"Are you?" she asked on a halting note, as if she'd expected him to fall into paroxysms of joy at the news.

"You hurt a lot of people to be with him, so I guess it's a shame it was all for nothing."

Christ, now she was weeping. She tried to cover it up, but not very well. "I think he wants his ex-wife back. I guess you think I deserve it."

Great. But at least he managed to avoid the bait she threw out. "Did he say he wanted her back?"

"No. Just a feeling I get, and I can't stand it anymore. Who do you have coming over?"

"A friend. Don't worry about it." Kelsey would probably fly through the roof when she found out about this. He wouldn't tell her, not tonight.

"You mean it's none of my business."

"If that's the way you want to take it."

"A girl?"

"Believe it or not, I didn't put my life on hold waiting for you to make this call, Courtney."

"I didn't think you were seeing anyone."

"I'm not. But I need to go right now. I've got stuff to do."

"Can we talk later?"

"What is there to talk about? There's nothing left to say that we haven't both already said a thousand times. You told me you were sorry. I told you I've forgiven you and I meant it. So if it's guilt you feel, don't beat yourself up. It happened. It's over and done with."

He'd forgiven her, sure. Forgiven her simply because he didn't give a damn anymore.

"I can't forgive *myself.*" Her voice was quivering, barely

discernible over the music from Brian's room. He covered his free ear with one hand.

"Then that's something you need to work on. I can't help you there."

"Tomorrow was supposed to be our wedding day. Remember?"

He nearly choked. Of course, he remembered. How could he forget how close he'd come to making the biggest mistake of his life? "Yes. Why are you bringing all this up?"

"I don't know. But sometimes I wish things were the way they used to be, and that I was still marrying you tomorrow. I messed up so bad. I know I need to make some changes." Her soft weeping had dampened, but he could hear it starting up again. "I'm so sorry I did this to us."

"You know who really deserves your apology? The one person who never got one. Kelsey."

"I can't talk to her. There's no way I could face her."

"And she might very well not want to face you. But it's something you should think about, on this path to betterment you're talking about. Now I mean it, I have to go."

She finally hung up, and he breathed a huge sigh of relief. Damn girl was depressing the hell out of him. And to think she wanted to come over tonight and drive the knife deeper. Remind him of all the ugliness. Perish the thought.

Of course, in her own way Kelsey would serve as a reminder of everything that happened. Her quiet heartbreak was palpable. But the strength behind it was a freaking inspiration to him. She hadn't backed down, she hadn't run back home even though her parents lived two states away. He loved to see that quality in someone, be it his dear friend or the people he stood up for in court.

He rushed through food prep so he could grab a quick shower before she arrived, since he was probably redolent with the lingering odor of huge, slobbering dog. It didn't surprise him how excited he was to see her; he always was. But now there was just a hint of scandal and possibility there that had his heartbeat ratcheting up a notch. It might be wrong, but it was undeniable.

They'd never lost touch throughout the years and her disastrous marriage, but they'd lost the closeness they once shared. He looked forward to gaining it back now without jealous significant others questioning their every conversation.

Even if Todd had come to realize what a jackass he'd been, he didn't deserve Kelsey after what he'd done to her. He hoped she realized that.

A vigorous shower later Evan headed back outside to fire up his grill beside the glowing kidney-shaped pool. It was a gorgeous night, still and musical with the sound of crickets. He lived far enough from the lights of town that every visible star winked from the expanse of velvety black sky unfurled above, but the late July humidity hung in the air like a sopping wet blanket. He was going around lighting the tiki torches when Brian stuck his head out the sliding glass door. "She's pulling up."

"And you're still here." Evan swept past him on his way into the kitchen.

"Lay off. I'm going over to Michelle's. I just got her on her cell and she won't be home for another half hour or so."

Evan swept a glance around the kitchen, rubbing palms that had become strangely damp on his jeans. Thank God Friday was the day his housekeeper came by. Everything was clean. Not that he ever let it get dirty. "That girl hasn't come to her senses yet?"

Brian perched on a barstool. "You'd better hope she doesn't. Where else would I go?"

"Good point." Satisfied that everything was presentable, Evan headed into the living room just as the doorbell rang. Reaching for the knob, he blew out a breath and pulled the door open.

Kelsey stood framed by the buttery glow of his porch light, smiling at him, looking delicious in denim shorts and a little pink top with spaghetti straps. Her dark hair—naturally curly, he knew—fell in a straight cascade from her white headband. "Hey," he drawled with a grin, holding his arms open.

She flew across the threshold to hug him, and God, she was so insubstantial in his arms. The tremor that went through her as he pressed her against him couldn't have been his imagination. Her familiar scent flooded his nostrils—she always smelled like cool spring breezes, like honeysuckle. Clean and sweet.

"I missed you," she said softly and, though the top of her head only reached his chin, he heard that voice as if it had whispered in his ear.

This was right. This was how they should be. He vowed in that moment to never let anyone come between them again.

"I missed you, too," he murmured, and when he finally went to release her, he realized he'd picked her up off her feet. He eased her down, staring into her gray eyes as if he hadn't seen them in years. It felt that way, for some reason. The trembling smile she was wearing for him didn't seem to reach the melancholy in her gaze. That sadness wasn't as pronounced as it had been at her divorce hearing almost two months ago—that had nearly torn his heart out—but it was still there.

As he shut the door she stepped back, looking him up and down. "You look great."

"Not as great as you." He put an arm around her shoulders and walked her through his living room toward the kitchen. Brian looked up and grinned as they entered.

"What's up, K?"

"Brian!"

"Don't worry, Evan's giving me the boot. I'll be gone in

a few."

"Well, I'm glad you're here now, because I have something to ask you."

Evan looked down at Kelsey in surprise as she left his side and walked over to his brother, who'd raised one dark, pierced brow in inquiry. And Evan could only see her from the back, but surely she wasn't doing what it looked like—which was raising her shirt up just an inch or two in front of Brian. "Does this thing look okay? It was doing fine, but now it's a little red and it bothers me. I'm afraid it's getting infected or something."

What the hell?

Brian, suddenly in his element, leaned down to examine what looked like the area around Kelsey's navel. "Nah. It's fine, just keep up your routine. It can take months to heal and it'll be a little red until it does."

Dumbfounded, Evan stepped around to see for himself. She'd gotten her bellybutton pierced, a silver barbell with a little butterfly on it. It was hot as hellfire. "When did you do that?" he asked.

She grinned at him. "The night my divorce was final. Brian did it for me."

Evan slapped the top of Brian's head. "You didn't tell me."

"Because I respect my clients' confidentiality. I do what they tell me. Who they show it to is their prerogative. Ass."

And she certainly hadn't minded showing it to Evan. He bit his lip on a grin as she turned to him. "I just felt like I needed to do something crazy…or crazy for me, anyway," she explained, lowering her shirt. Todd probably wouldn't have gone for it, he thought. "Lisa went with me."

Brian burst out laughing. "Yeah, the pregnant chick. She was hilarious. You were fine afterward, but I thought she was about to pass out on the floor."

"And she's the one who's gone through the rigors of childbirth twice already. I didn't let her live it down, don't worry," Kelsey said. Brian held out his fist and she bumped her knuckles against his, laughing.

Evan shook his head. "I'm still reeling from the fact that you willingly let *my brother* drive a needle through your flesh."

"It was a very liberating moment," she told him with a dead-straight face.

"See? These are the rewards of my profession," Brian said to Evan. "Giving hot chicks their first taste of the wild life. We love to get our hands on virgin flesh in my line of work."

"You're twisted," Evan said, and it didn't escape him that Kelsey was laughing good-naturedly but covering her mouth with her hand and flushing bright red to the roots of her hair.

He shifted the conversation before she could somehow bolt. "Yeah, you love it when you go *do* your line of work."

Brian popped the tab on the beer that had been sitting next to him. "They love *me* so much there, I can come and go as I please. Much like Michelle. Speaking of which, I'm out." He rose from his barstool and grabbed his keys from the counter. "You kids have fun. Don't do—"

"Not with that." Evan gestured toward the can in Brian's hand. "Open container law. You do this on purpose to bait me, don't you?"

"Jesus Christ. You're such a *lawyer*." Brian always spat the word as if it were a curse.

"That may be, but right now I'm big brother and you're not leaving my house drinking. Wait till you get to Michelle's. Hand it over."

Kelsey was watching the heated exchange with her eyebrows in her hairline. But she'd get used to it, if she hung around the two of them for any length of time. If she really wanted to see ugliness, she should watch Evan's older sister lay into Brian. Or his mother, who reverted to Italian when she was really pissed off.

"Fine." Brian shoved the beer into Evan's hands. "Enjoy with my compliments, you rat bastard."

"I surely will, since it's *mine*."

Brian flipped him off as he exited through the patio door.

"Well," Kelsey said in the silence that followed, during which they both stared at the door where he had disappeared. "That was…"

"Minor. Trust me. Sorry you had to witness it." He took a swig of Brian's abandoned beer and walked around the counter to the refrigerator. "Want a drink?"

God, did she ever. If anyone had told her a month ago this would be happening, Kelsey would have accused them of being insane. "Sure."

"Margaritas?"

"Sounds good."

He set to work making them and she took a moment, as always, to envy him his kitchen. It was a hodgepodge of rugged brick, wrought-iron scrollwork and stainless steel, making her think of an old Italian bistro with plenty of modern upgrades. She loved this entire house. A log-cabin style with pale, naked wood walls and hardwood floors, it wasn't too big, wasn't too small…just right for him. And maybe one other person, of course. It had two bedrooms downstairs and a loft that overlooked the living room—he used the upstairs as his home office. It was filled with law books. Right now she had a couple of quilts her great-grandmother had made that would look gorgeous hanging over the loft railing. It was a crime they were bagged up in her closet, but she had nowhere to display them that did justice to their beauty or their preciousness to her.

I'm redecorating his house in my head. Crazy, girl. Crazy.

He'd bought the place shortly after proposing to Courtney and they'd lived here around eighteen months before she decided she liked Kelsey's life better. For whatever reason.

Now *that* was a crazy girl.

Evan looked incredibly edible tonight—she couldn't recall ever thinking he didn't. He was wearing a pair of worn, faded jeans, and he was owning them. A white polo shirt hugged his broad shoulders, so stark and sexy set against his olive complexion and his raven-black hair. Hair that was still damp and redolent from a recent shower. She could spend her entire day doing nothing more than inhaling his scent. Or staring at that ass. It was one fine ass. What she wouldn't give to feel it bare and cupped in her hands, urging him deeper...

God. Hopefully he would think her full-body blush was still from Brian's ribbing. What had she been thinking wearing this top? She must be splotchy all over. Maybe she needed to rethink some of the clothes she'd packed, as well.

He finished making her margarita, and even the first few sips made her head swim a bit. It had been too long. She wasn't much of a drinker, though she indulged on special occasions. And tonight would definitely count.

"Do you need any help?" she offered, though he seemed to have it all well under control.

He smiled on his way out to the grill with a platter. "Nope, but you can come outside with me."

They sat poolside while she nursed her margarita and he drank a longneck, watching the moon's slow climb into the heavens. A scrumptious aroma drifted over from the grill, mingling with the summery scent of chlorine and citronella. God, she could get used to this. But it wasn't long before her clothes were sticking to her and she was tempted to dive headfirst into his pool to escape the heat. As soon as the steaks were done, they went back into the bliss of the air conditioning.

Kelsey wandered into his living room with every pretense of sitting and relaxing, but really she just wanted to survey the environment he dwelled in post-Courtney. She'd never seen it without the other woman's influence.

She hadn't had very much, it seemed. The furniture was the same, as were the decorative pictures on the walls. What *had* changed, she noticed with a slow spread of warmth in her chest, was the addition of a few pictures of Evan and Kelsey together.

Laughing at a party, arm in arm. Hugging at their graduation wearing their caps and gowns. She'd been crying just before that picture was taken because she was a sap like that. But it had been the end of an era for her—a fun one—and quite scary to contemplate moving with Todd to a strange town. Evan had come home with them, though he'd been busy most of the summer getting ready to move to Austin to start law school. Thank goodness he had come back here once he was done, when he could have gone anywhere he wanted.

"These are great," she said when she heard him enter the room behind her.

"The good ol' days."

"You didn't have the pictures here before. I guess Courtney didn't like them."

"Sometimes it's just easier to keep the peace, you know?"

She laughed, but there was no humor in it. "Tell me about it."

"So what's been going on with you? I haven't seen you in a couple of months."

"The usual. Work. Volunteering. Not much else."

"Been seeing anybody?"

The question surprised her. "No."

"Surely not from lack of offers, though." He winked at

her as he took a drink of his beer.

"Well, I have been asked out a couple of times. I just didn't feel up to it yet. What about you?" She thought she knew the answer, but feared she might be wrong.

He waved a dismissive hand. "Been flying solo all this time. Can you believe it?"

Given his track record? No, she couldn't. Ever since she'd known him he hadn't gone more than a month between girlfriends. "I guess it's a good thing to take some time to yourself…" She trailed off and scoffed, then laughed miserably. "What the hell am I saying? I *hate* it."

Evan nodded, not taking his gaze from her. "Yeah, me too."

He missed Courtney. He had to, even if pride wouldn't allow him to say it. Even if he wouldn't admit it around her, knowing how she felt about the woman.

"You know, it's okay if you want to talk about all that," she began, her voice more tentative than she would have liked. "I mean if you need to get something out or whatever. I know sometimes it doesn't seem like I can take it without going off, but I can. I just want you to know I'm here for you. I don't want you to think there are things you can't say to me. We've always been able to talk about anything and everything, and I don't want that to change."

There. The spiel was out. Hopefully it had knocked the first dent in the wall that had sprung up between them last Christmas. She couldn't stand its presence anymore. They hadn't asked for this, it had been done to them.

"I appreciate that, and I want you to know the same goes for me." He gave her a look she felt all the way down to her toes. "You're incredible, you know that?"

She shook her head. "Nah."

"Yes. I mean it. I know you can take it, Kelsey. You can take anything anyone dishes out. You're stronger than you give yourself credit for."

It was nice to hear, but it left a messy splat where her heart used to be, because he was so wrong about her. She wasn't the girl he'd known in college. *That* girl had been resilient. She'd had to be, to nurture all that unrequited love for Evan and still be able to face seeing him every day. To find the strength to finally let go and redirect it to someone else.

But look where it had gotten her.

By the time all the food was ready, she was parked on the leather sofa, nearly full on tortilla chips and hot sauce. He made the best salsa that had ever crossed her lips, lots of cilantro, the way she liked it.

"This stuff is amazing, as usual," she called, popping another chip in her mouth. The dip was a little spicier than she liked and she'd been relying rather heavily on the pitcher of margaritas to dampen the sting—of both her downward-spiraling emotions and the sauce. She was lucky the latter wasn't worse. Evan wanted almost everything he ate to be four-alarm.

He grinned as he brought their plates in from the kitchen. She would've helped him, but the room seemed to tilt a bit whenever she stood. "Come over more often, and I'll spring some of my mom's recipes on you," he told her.

"I can't believe you like to cook so much."

He sat beside her, handing her a plate. She had to repress a fidget as his left knee pressed against her right, his heat suffusing her. And she was already hot enough as it was, flushed with tequila. She hated to eat in here, afraid she'd make a mess in her clumsy state, but he'd insisted it was fine. He had several seasons of *Seinfeld* on DVD and since they had always been addicts—and Todd and Courtney had hated the show—a marathon was in order. "I don't mind it," he said. "Besides, if I didn't cook, Brian might starve to death."

"Speaking of, you two are the very definition of 'polar

opposites.' Not that I even have to tell you that."

"Yeah, it's like all the drive and ambition in the family ran out after me."

"I think it's nice that you look out for him, though. He needs you, whether he admits it or not."

"He frustrates me. He's got potential, he just doesn't care. We had to threaten him with everything under the sun to even get him to finish high school. I worry about him."

In profile she could see the tight set of his jaw. She really didn't know what to say to comfort him about that.

Yep, college all over again. She cut vigorously into her steak and popped a juicy piece into her mouth. Evan hadn't lost his touch. Steak sauce would be an abomination on this. He'd baked potatoes, too, and hers was piled high with butter, cheese and sour cream. She couldn't even begin to discern everything that topped his. But she would lay bets it wouldn't put an ounce on his frame.

He was watching her chew. "I remembered that you don't like it too spicy, so I went easy on yours," he said. "I hope it's all right."

"It's perfect," she assured him. It seemed to practically melt in her mouth. He was awesome. There was nothing he couldn't do.

"Well, there're a few things, I guess."

Oh, crap, had she spoken out loud? She'd have to watch that, only open her mouth to insert food. Yeah, right. The margaritas were just too good.

An hour passed…or two or more, she wasn't sure, she just knew they demolished pretty much everything in his kitchen and her glass kept getting empty and Evan kept pressing in closer and closer at her side—or maybe she was leaning on him. They were still laughing at each other and the hilarity ensuing on his plasma screen, but her clothes had become such an irritating scrape against her heated flesh she could hardly cope.

She blew out a breath and tugged at her shirt, trying to pull it away from her sensitized breasts, but that didn't alleviate the friction her damn strapless bra was causing across her nipples. She stretched, arching her back and rolling her head on her shoulders. When she stopped, the room kept rolling. Or maybe her head was still moving. She couldn't tell. She just knew it was damn funny.

Evan watched Kelsey giggle as she tried in vain to get control of her neck muscles. A sense of dread was fast overtaking his thoughts. "Are you okay?" he asked after a moment, and the question shocked her eyes fully open.

"Sure am. Why wouldn't I be?"

"Because I realize now that pitcher of 'ritas I made is just about empty."

"Ohhhh…'m sorry, didja want more? Is my head moving?"

Yep. Blitzed. She'd probably be puking in no time. "No and yes. Kelsey, how long has it been since you had anything to drink?"

She giggled again. She was doing a lot of that. Her eyes closed. "Dunno. Can't remember. Long time."

"Looks like you can't hold your liquor, honey."

Her brows drew together, her lips forming a perfect pout. She cracked open one eye to peer up at him. "I can too lick my holder."

Evan burst into laughter and pulled her against him. She was damn near dead weight. *Party's over.* "I bet you can. Come on, up we go." When he stood, she flopped over on the couch without him there to support her. He slid one arm under her back and his other behind her knees. She grumbled incoherently when he lifted her… Christ, she was featherlight in his arms. He was glad he'd shoveled food down her all night. Now if she could just hang on to it. He should have noticed the gradual depletion of the pitcher of margaritas.

One small lamp in a far corner was the only illumination in his bedroom as he carried her inside cradled in his arms. The clock on his nightstand told him in glowing red that it was a quarter till three. Kelsey snuggled into his chest, and he tried to ignore the smoothness of her bare legs across his forearm. Like warm, tantalizing silk. He sat her on his bed, supporting her weight as he pulled back the comforter. Still, she managed to escape his grip and began to topple backward.

"Whoa," he laughed, reaching for her as her eyes popped open and she grabbed for him before she could land. "I got you."

"Evan," she murmured, wrapping her soft arms around his neck. Their position had her lips near his ear. She'd lost her headband somewhere. He could smell the strawberry of her shampoo, feel the tickle of her sluggish breath stirring his hair. "Evan."

"Move over here, lie down."

She pulled back slightly, her bleary eyes trying to focus on his. The weight of her head still seemed too much for her neck to support and her hair flowed over his arm. "Evan, I always liked you."

"I always liked you, too, honey." The way she kept saying his name in that intoxicated purr, savoring the *v* between her teeth and her bottom lip, was unnerving. Unnerving, hell. It had his dick twitching in his pants. "Come on, girl, you need to sleep it off."

"I mean I *like* liked you."

Shit. Most people who uttered careless words while drunk tended to blame it on the alcohol later. He'd always found it to be the time when the truth came out. Danger signals were going off in his brain. "You're drunk. Sleep."

Though she was most likely oblivious to his commands, he didn't like how desperate his voice was starting to sound to his own ears.

"No I'm not." Her silly lopsided grin belied her words as she finally obeyed his coaxing and crawled to the spot he'd cleared. He pulled the covers up for her as she settled against the pillow and peered up at him. The heat in her eyes as she did so damn near destroyed him. "I don' wanna sleep." She kicked, flinging the covers off just as he got them arranged. "Don' need all that, I'm hot. I'm too hot."

Was she ever. He raked a hand through his hair. For such a little thing, her legs seemed to go on forever, long and sleek. He could only imagine the silken glide her inner thighs would be against his fingertips. Her shirt had ridden up to bare her flat midriff, where her belly ring winked at him in the dim lighting—damn, that was sexy, and so out of place on her. Her breasts strained against the tight little shirt, and the friction had her nipples peaking beneath the fabric.

Her hands caught his face, surprising him. He should have moved away from her long ago, before she could get her hands on him. As it was, he felt like a fly caught in the sticky gossamer of a spider's den. "Always wanted to fuck you, y'know that? Even when I was a virgin."

He drew in a breath, exhaled it shakily. So much for prudish.

Note to self: Kelsey now gets unbelievably horny when drunk.

She licked her lips, staring into his eyes with surprising clarity for someone who had nearly passed out moments ago. The glint of moisture her tongue left behind was mesmerizing. He wanted to taste it. The heat of her palms sank into his flesh. She was burning up. Her legs were haphazardly parted, still tangled in the covers, and he could scent her arousal, musky and sweet.

"It's not going to happen, Kelsey." His voice probably sounded as firm as a little girl's, but he gave it his best shot.

All his strength had drained to his dick. It pushed against his zipper until he thought it might burst through if he didn't release it soon. "You've had too much to drink."

That pout resurfaced, but he was astounded at the pain that leaked into her gray eyes. It was…real, and raw, not some byproduct of an inebriated mind.

"You don' want me. Why'd you never want me?" She was rubbing her thighs together now, the action only causing her scent to waft stronger into his nostrils. Like witchcraft, it drew him toward her, made the mental filmstrip of tearing her shorts off and sinking himself into the tight wet heat of her pussy play over and over again in his head until it obliterated all else: morals, rationale, sanity. And he had never wanted her. Right.

God, she would feel so good closing in around him. He'd deprived himself for too long. She took one of his hands and laid it flat on her belly, then pushed it down toward the place she needed it. Her stomach muscles pulled taut beneath his reluctant touch, and that skin was hot and satiny. She leaned upward, parting her lush pink lips in wanton invitation.

No.

It was one thing for two people to get hammered and go at each other. It was quite another when one of them had full control of his faculties and the other had none. Criminal even, and he could never take advantage of her like that. But he'd never been quite so tempted, he had to give her that much.

He pulled his hand away from hers and went to stand. She emitted some incoherent whimper that ripped at his heart, completely decimating it when the sound formed into words. "Evan, don't leave…don't leave me like this…please…"

No other hetero male on the planet could have endured the sight of her all disheveled in his bed, writhing and senseless and begging him to fuck her, without falling on her like a rutting animal. He should be declared saint of all the world to have lasted this long. If he hadn't known her for all these years, he couldn't have stopped himself.

Beads of sweat had formed on her forehead; one trickled back into her hair. The skin above her neckline glistened in the soft lighting. She was in flames, and he'd hardly put a hand on her.

"Kelsey, don't do this to me."

"Please," she whispered again, gazing up at him, utterly smashed but still capable of all the determined longing that came along with such a state. She wouldn't let herself pass out until she got it. "*Do* something. Touch me. Evan. God, I need it."

The husky plea pushed him past his breaking point. She sounded like a different woman. He couldn't give her everything she wanted, but if he could satisfy her without losing his mind, maybe she would pass out.

"Take off your shorts," he whispered, knowing with brutal certainty that he was going to hell. The only consolation was the hope that she wouldn't remember anything in the morning. He knew her, and she would be mortified. But if she did remember...well, they would deal with it. "I'll make it better."

Her fingers were frantic and clumsy, and he had to help her. When she at last kicked the denim from her foot, the sight and scent of her drenched pink panties caused him physical anguish. She hooked her thumbs in the sides of the frothy lace, but he stilled her hand as he moved to lie beside her. He slid one arm beneath her head. "No, sweetie. Lie back."

"But—"

"Shhh."

She did as he told her but she mewled disconsolately about it. He fortified himself with a deep breath and slid his fingers under that sinful lace. He should have stayed on top of it. He'd meant to, but he had to allow himself this one thing.

The feel of her. Heaven was under there, dewy curls and soft, hot, creamy folds. Kelsey threw her head back on his arm and moaned as his fingertips grazed her, her legs falling open to give him the full feel and scent of her. The graceful arc of her neck was something to behold, a sculptor's wet dream.

His cock throbbed as he deliberately avoided venturing lower to the source of her wetness — the feel of that might well send him over the edge, plunge him into a madness that could only end with him spending himself inside of her. And damn her, she kept lifting her hips, trying to force his touch lower. He fought her, strumming her clit, caressing and stroking, slow and light to quick and hard. All the while he watched her face soften into that exquisite feminine expression of impending ecstasy, lips open, eyes closed, brows drawing together. Gorgeous.

"Take off my panties and lick me," she whispered urgently.

"No. Just this."

"Dammit!" she cried. "Don't be like *him*."

He didn't have to guess who she meant, and just for that, he wanted to throw her thighs over his shoulders and tongue that tight little bud until she screamed for mercy.

Later. She was drunk on tequila and lust and he couldn't let her bait him now. The trip was looking more and more delicious to him.

Kelsey came against his fingers with a ferocity that almost killed him. She seized his shoulders, her fingernails biting into his flesh through his shirt as her body tightened and she thrust her hips in rhythm with his hand. Her cries rang throughout his house, that usually gentle voice bold and carnal as it cried out his name, called him endearments. It was a sound he wouldn't mind hearing again and again, shattering this emptiness, and he answered it with senseless murmurings in her ear, groaning with his need to feel her rippling and clenching around him.

The tension had no sooner flowed out of her than she was

snoring, her arms slipping from around his neck. He couldn't repress a chuckle, though his hard-on made it difficult to contemplate the fact that she was out now and he was alone in the same anguish she had just suffered.

Evan crawled away from her side and retrieved her shorts from the floor. There really was no danger of waking her at this point, so he slid them back over her legs, fastened them and threw the covers over her again. Her dark hair curtained her face. He reached down and gently drew the strands away, dropping a soft kiss to her forehead.

"Damn," he whispered. He liked the look of her cuddled under his blankets, in his bed. He liked her hair spread out on his pillow. Her skin was pale and stark against the burgundy sheets and a twinge of worry, of aching tenderness for her, sparked in his chest. She'd been through so much, and he feared she wasn't over it yet. He also feared he was the one who'd stirred it all up for her again.

It was irrational, but he couldn't shake this constant lingering feeling that some of the blame for the entire debacle was on his shoulders. He'd introduced her to her ex-husband eight years ago, entrusting Todd with the girl who'd been a better friend to him in a couple of years than Todd had been since they were kids.

Sighing, he turned away and grimaced as he ambled toward his closet with the unyielding denim of his jeans playing hell on his erection. He retrieved an extra blanket and pillow and went to make his own bed, on the couch. What he wanted was to crawl under the covers next to Kelsey and hold her in his arms all through the night.

Evan was yawning at the kitchen counter and pouring another cup of strong black coffee when the unmistakable sound of retching drifted in from the direction of his room. He was surprised she'd made it this long.

He rubbed a hand over his eyes. He'd spent all night dreaming about her sweetness against his fingers, even after taking a shower as cold as he could stand it and coming hard in his hand with her name ricocheting through his brain. It had been a fitful sleep, to say the least, and he hadn't even been able to go for his run this morning to work off the lingering frustration. Rain had begun to fall just after dawn—he'd still been lying awake—and it didn't appear to be letting up anytime soon. Ordinarily he would've just run through it and been thankful for the relief in this heat, but not with Kelsey here to look after.

Rain on what was supposed to be his wedding day. That would've sent Courtney into a screeching tailspin. Thank God he didn't have to listen to it, although he could almost hear it. *Oh my God, Evan! My dress! My hair! My makeup! Make it stop!*

Well, she hadn't been quite that bad. But somehow she probably would have made him feel like it was his fault water was falling from the sky.

He took a bottle of water out of his fridge, anticipating Kelsey's cotton-mouth, and walked into his bedroom half afraid of what he would find. She'd flung the covers halfway across the room and his bathroom door was partially closed, as if she'd made a halfhearted attempt to slam it behind her on her mad dash. He walked over and rapped on it with his knuckles.

"You all right?"

"Ugghhhh," was the response. He shook his head, smirking as he watched the rain drool down the windowpane across the room. Dim, murky gray light filtered over everything. She was lucky in that regard. No blinding morning sun to assault her senses.

He dared to push the door open a bit and peek inside. She was lying on the floor, her cheek pressed against the tiles, her skin as white as they were. Oh, he'd been there before. Those tiles were very cool to the touch, especially against flushed skin.

Her eyes opened a bit, and she moaned when she saw him standing there. "I sure hate to tell you to go away in your own house."

He laughed, walking in despite her words. "That's right. You can't." He opened his medicine cabinet and got her a couple of Tylenol, which he handed to her after unscrewing the lid of the water bottle for her. "Here."

"Thanks." She pushed herself up on one arm and gulped it down like she was a lost desert traveler, delicate throat muscles contracting. Half the bottle of water drained before she stopped. She wiped her mouth, put the bottle on the floor and lay back down. "Just let me stay here, please."

He leaned over, meaning to drag her up to her feet. "Not an option. You can't be comfortable down there."

"I'm so sorry."

He froze, swallowing hard. She was looking up at him with a wretchedness in her eyes he could only interpret to be guilt or profound regret. She must remember.

"For what?"

"For passing out on you like that. I don't normally act like this, I promise. I'll get out of your hair in a few minutes—"

Relief bore down hard on him and he knelt down next to her. Guilt was tearing him up that he'd touched her at all in that state. He should have been able to walk away, and in the harsh light of day, he couldn't believe how weak he was. "Stop that talk, you can stay all day if you want. And I know how you act. I'm sorry for letting you get to that point."

"Today is supposed to be your wedding day, isn't it?" she asked softly. Her voice was hoarse.

"Yeah. Some weather we would've had, huh?"

"Really, I'll go in just a minute, I don't mean to—"

"Shh. Do you think I want to spend my rainy would-be wedding day by myself?" He grinned at her. "Hang out with me."

She must've been convinced, because she smiled back. "Did I walk to bed or did you have to carry me?"

He tugged the collar of his T-shirt, though it wasn't what was about to choke him. "I carried you."

She covered her eyes with one hand. "You probably don't want to go anywhere with me now."

"Yes I do." *More than ever.* "I can't wait to go away with you."

A trembling smile touched her lips, causing his chest to ache. Even wound tight in a fetal position on his bathroom floor, sick and ashen with finger-in-light-socket hair, she was beautiful to him. The need to take care of her roared through him, the desire to take away the pain. He cleared his throat. "What do you feel like? If you want to take a shower, I'll see if I can scrounge up something you can wear after."

"Okay," she said after seeming to seriously debate it with herself.

"Come on." He reached for her again, and she let him, curling her slender fingers around his biceps as he drew her to her feet. When he determined she was steady enough, he reached into his shower and turned on the water. "Towels are behind you there in that cabinet. Sorry if all my soap and stuff is too manly-smelling for you." Some of Courtney's leftover stuff probably still lurked in the depths of his cabinets, but he doubted Kelsey wanted to smell like the woman who'd ruined her marriage.

She chuckled. "It's okay. I'll probably just stand there and soak for about three hours."

"However long you need." The urge to stroke her face,

touch her hair, was compelling, along with the need to do a number of other things to her. Knowing she was about to be naked in his shower was torture enough without the memory of last night, the way she'd smelled, the way she'd felt. "I'll be right back."

He left to rummage through his drawers, trying to dispel the images. Finally he located a pair of sweats she could pin at the waist and roll up if she had to. One of his UT Law T-shirts and she'd be fairly set, though it would hang to her knees. He took it all into the bathroom and left it folded on the counter.

She was sitting on the closed toilet lid now, her head between her knees as steam billowed from the shower stall.

"You okay?" he asked. "I can run you a bath, if you'd rather not stand."

"I'll be all right," she said weakly, sitting up straight again. "Just nauseated."

"I'll leave you alone. When you're done I have coffee in the kitchen, if you feel like it. Yell if you need anything. I mean it, Kelsey. You remember college. I've had to babysit the drunk many times before. You're a picnic, if only because I can pick you up if I have to." He grinned at her, and she managed to return it.

"Thank you. I will." She looked him in the eye, and her sincerity and embarrassment tugged him in all the right places. He felt for her. He couldn't stand being sick in other people's presence, either.

Closing the door behind him, he thought about what he'd gotten himself into. If one night with her had him in such pitiful shape, one week might very well kill him.

Damn. She'd been something else last night. He didn't think he could put himself through it again. If it had been the truth…shit, what he wouldn't give to see Kelsey like that, crazed and begging him for it, out of her mind with lust for him without alcohol sharpening those base urges. Why the hell did they have to have so much history in the way? He was torn between the guilt of touching her at all and the insanity of wishing he'd spent all damn night in her silky heat. So that she wouldn't have to go home today not knowing about that one sweet interlude.

He wanted her to tell him *sober* what she had admitted to so freely last night.

Chapter Four

Evan had always thought he'd never seen Kelsey look more beautiful than on her wedding day. He'd stood beside Todd and watched her slow approach, a dream in white, lacking only wings to complete the angelic image she'd made. If his jaw had been clenched in misery and his hands nearly shaking, no one noticed, because all eyes had been on her, and hers on Todd.

As best man Evan had stood in support of the union, toasted the bride and groom to a lifetime of happiness, and laughed and danced with Kelsey and her bridesmaids, all the while suffering from an aching void where his heart once resided. A gnawing ache that perhaps he'd let a good thing slip right through his fingers. He'd witnessed the girl he should never have let get away vow to love his best friend, until death—or Courtney, as it turned out—parted them.

Today, it was all made right. She might have been a soft, ethereal vision on her wedding day binding herself to another man, but out here beneath the kiss of the Hawaiian sun, she was a bronzed goddess, and just for now, she was all his.

"This is *amazing*," she groaned from her prone position on a beach towel in the sand. Her voice was almost carnal, causing stirrings it wouldn't do for Evan to exhibit in public. He'd made it through rubbing lotion over her silken back, so he could make it through her well-contented purrs. She turned her face toward him. "Thank you so much for this."

She was thanking *him* when she was wearing that bikini?

The wind blew in off the jewel-blue waves as he let his gaze roam freely over her: the tossed curls of her dark brown ponytail, the clean lines of her oiled body glistening in the sun, the swelling curve of her ass hidden under a triangular scrap of pink and white fabric. This was really the most he'd ever seen of her body, but he could tell she still hadn't begun to replace the weight she'd lost since the divorce, weight she really couldn't afford to lose in the first place. It didn't matter to him how she looked—he couldn't remember a time when he hadn't thought she was ravishing. But it never failed to start the slow burn of anger to think she'd been so stressed and hurt that she hadn't been taking care of herself like she should.

If her storm-gray eyes were open behind the dark sunglasses she wore, she could see he was looking at her. But his own blacked-out shades hid exactly where he was looking.

"I'm glad you're having a good time," he told her. "Like I said, you deserve it."

Her lips curled as the wind cast one tendril from her ponytail across her face. She swiped it away, lifting her head and propping herself on her elbows. He couldn't tear his gaze from the way her generous breasts stretched her bikini top in that position. Just one hook of his finger and he could finally know the color of their luscious tips.

"What are we doing tonight?" she asked, a weighted question if ever there was one.

"You want to just take it easy? Hang out?" he asked.

Their flight had landed Sunday afternoon and it was Tuesday. Yesterday they'd hiked to the Diamond Head crater and marveled at the breathtaking panorama around them. He'd seen it before, but Kelsey's enthusiasm had been so infectious it was almost like seeing it for the first time. Today, they'd just wanted to laze out on the beach. Thank God she was a more laid-back vacationer. He hated to come home from a trip more exhausted than when he'd left—what was the point then? But there was a lot more he wanted to show her.

Against her tan, her teeth were dazzlingly white. "Sure. I could use a drink, though."

Oh *hell*. He pushed his sunglasses to the top of his head and shot her a look. She laughed. "Don't worry, I won't pass out on you again. We're on vacation, right? Just a couple of margaritas."

"Sure, that we can manage. Sounds good to me, too. Then we can come back in and order room service."

"Ahhh. Divine."

He grinned at her and sent up probably the hundredth prayer of thanks that he was here with Kelsey and not his ex on some sham of a honeymoon. Courtney could probably make some guy a happy man one day. She was smart and beautiful, certainly no fluff piece of arm candy. She was his younger brother's age but already ran her own business—a downtown boutique his mom frequented—and it was there he'd met her for the first time. His mother still couldn't convince him there weren't ulterior motives involved the day she called and asked him if he'd stop by the store and pay on her account. Courtney had been working that day. He'd asked her out on the spot. His mom knew him too well.

She'd managed to fit right in with his sometimes overwhelming, boisterous family. But like all the others, she just wasn't the one for him. Though she'd perhaps come closest.

He often wondered if they'd have made it to the altar even if she hadn't been unfaithful. She'd presented him with an easy out, and he'd pounced on it. He wondered what Kelsey would say when she heard Courtney and Todd had split up.

Ordinarily, Evan wouldn't have given a damn what happened to Todd Jacobs. He wouldn't have wasted a single thought on the bastard if there hadn't been ramifications for Kelsey. If Courtney was to be believed, any day now Todd could come crawling back to Kelsey. The thought made his blood seethe. He wanted to talk to her about it, ask her how she felt, but she was having too much fun to dredge up that stuff, and he figured if he asked her she would give an answer that was automatic instead of genuine. But if, *if* Todd showed up at her door, would she listen to his excuses and take him back?

Evan didn't think so, but he didn't know. She seemed to carry a lot of guilt over the fact that her marriage had failed, regardless that it was not of her doing. Guilt could be a bitch of a motivator.

Kelsey followed him in for a quick dip in the waves before they collected their beach gear and headed for their ridiculously lavish suite. His parents certainly hadn't spared any expense, probably a testament to how desperate they were to marry him off.

But it seemed nothing could stop the intrusion of reality. For the second day in a row, there was a frantic message from Evan's legal assistant waiting on his BlackBerry.

He cursed when he saw the number, and Kelsey laughed. "Duty calls, even in paradise," she said, patting him on the shoulder as she slipped past him into the bathroom, surely to shower off all that sand from her glistening body. God, how he'd love to do it, he thought as he reluctantly called his assistant's personal cell to see what the hell had blown up at the office. Given the four-hour time difference, everyone would be home by now.

Even as Delilah finished updating him and started jabbering in his ear about God knew what, his mind kept going back to the image of Kelsey standing naked under the spray, her hands all over her body as she rinsed away the banana-scented oil adhering the grains of beach sand to her skin. And him running his tongue along her tan lines. Jesus. His cock began to swell inside his swimming trunks. If she came out now... *Shit.* He needed to go check baseball scores or something, anything to get those pictures out of his head.

He wiped his fingers hard over his eyes. "Delilah, I have to go. You guys have a good week. Call me if anything else comes up."

Plenty had come up here. Evan cut her off without waiting for a reply and drew a breath, resisting the urge to adjust himself because it would probably only make the situation worse to touch it. He sat hard on the bed and collapsed back on the mattress.

Not helping matters was his nearly undeniable suspicion Kelsey had masturbated right here in the bed next to him last night, thinking him asleep. He had been mindfucked on that one, a grown man not knowing what the hell to do with the enflamed, *sober* female next to him—turn over and help her out at the risk of embarrassing the hell out of his longtime friend, or let her finish, only to have to creep into the bathroom and take care of himself after she was asleep.

Like a dumbass, he'd chosen the latter. The thought of her fingertips slipping through her wet folds with gentle urgency, the memory of what it had felt like when he'd done the same, had his dick throbbing now like a smashed thumb. He wondered if it was him she fantasized about touching her as she came silently next to him. If she would've liked it if he *had* turned over and replaced her fingers with his own. If she'd have begged him to push his cock into her pussy, already wet and ready for him. If she would've cried his name into the darkness as she climaxed in his arms, no more need for silence.

Ten years ago there wouldn't have been a question. The girl had carried her soul in her eyes. She only had to look at him back then and he knew she could be his for the taking. But the sweetness and innocence he'd loved in her as a friend had been the very things that kept him away.

He'd been a double major in political science and criminal justice, president of too many damn clubs and honor societies to remember, all to bulk up his law school apps. He'd been a social animal, but he hadn't had time for anything more than superficial, shallow relationships with girls he knew were just passing through his life. He hadn't wanted to get derailed by love. And Kelsey, he knew, would have damn well derailed him. One taste of her and he feared he would have wandered around lost in a euphoric fog.

He hadn't been thinking fate would step in to keep her in his life all these years. But it had, and even worse, Kelsey's gray eyes had cooled over that time. Nothing there gave him any indication whether she still felt anything for him, just one drunken confession he wasn't entirely sure if he should believe or not. He was praying for s*omething* in there to reveal itself in the light of day, to let him know she really was susceptible to him.

Her giving in to a physical need and getting herself off within arm's reach of him still wasn't enough. Too much was at risk. She was driving him crazy, just like she always had. Why did their timing always have to be so off? If she still wasn't over Todd, he didn't want to get caught up in that baggage no matter what he felt for her.

Their friendship was far too precious for him to throw caution to the wind and offer her everything, only for her to leave him when her ex-husband showed up at her door full of apologies and promises.

Kelsey wiped the steam from the mirror with her towel and stared at her reflection. Her skin was flushed from the heat of her shower…or the wild sexual heat she'd been in ever since Evan showed up at her door to sweep her away to paradise.

"You're in a mess," she informed herself quietly, as if she didn't already know. The very mess she'd anticipated. Sighing, she grabbed her hairdryer, flipped her hair over and began to blow it dry.

She didn't want any more nights like last night and the one before. Upon first arrival Evan had offered to take the sofa in the living room, but she'd felt wretched about that, being this was his trip—his should-be *honeymoon*, she reminded herself. She'd offered to take it herself, and he flat refused. So lying next to him in what seemed like acres of bed, yearning for him yet unable to touch him, had twisted a dagger through her heart. She wanted to be in his arms, those strong, lean-muscled arms, and it was the very place she didn't need to go.

But damn, how her fantasies had evolved. In college they'd been filled with mushy romance and gentleness. Now, lying there eyeing the strong contours of his body next to her, all she could think about was him crawling over her, kneeing apart her thighs and pounding into her aching pussy like he owned it. Whispering in her ear things that were feverish and forbidden in between groans and wet, devouring kisses.

The images were so vivid given his nearness that she could almost feel him inside her. Which led to her own fingers seeking out the damp longing between her legs and trying to soothe that emptiness, if only superficially. Only he would be able to eradicate it for her altogether. She almost wished he would catch her in the naughty act. Almost.

Oh, God. She wondered what he would do if she worked up the nerve to just walk out of the bathroom naked and jump him. Drag him to bed. Have her way with him.

Stop! This was *Evan*. Best man at her wedding, as her mother had so graciously pointed out. How wrong was that?

Sighing, she switched off her hairdryer and quickly dressed. She knew he would be waiting to shower, so she didn't take any time to straighten her hair. The Hawaiian humidity would have its way with it anyway, tossing it into wild curls no matter what measures she took to prevent it.

She'd go easy on the drinks tonight for sure. One more drunken fantasy as vivid as the dream she'd had at his house that night and she'd be lost. Just thinking about it made the roots of her hair tingle, and in her dream he'd done nothing but touch her...and look at her as if she was the most beautiful, precious sight on earth.

That, she thought, had been the sweetest thing of all.

"Truth or dare!" Kelsey laughed hysterically, drawing glances from other patrons in the bar off the opulent lobby. She knew her and Evan's reminiscing was overriding the quiet, laid-back buzz of conversation around them, but she didn't care.

Evan laughed with her and signaled the waitress to bring them more margaritas. One more, he'd laughingly warned her a few minutes ago, and they were done. "We were the terror of many a party, playing a stupid grade-school game."

"That fight we staged," she recalled out loud. "We had rumors flying all night. One of them was that you'd knocked me up."

"I remember that! My girlfriend dumped me over it, and it was just a joke."

Kelsey hadn't liked that girl anyway, but she was able to

bite down on the sentiment for the sake of not pissing him off. Most of his girlfriends she'd been able to tolerate, even if she was envious beyond belief of them. They'd been beautiful and smart and nice to her—most of them, anyway—so what was not to like? No airhead bimbos for him. She'd only wanted to be where they were.

She and Courtney had never really made it beyond the obligatory our-men-are-best-friends-so-we-have-to-like-each-other relationship. They'd gone shopping together once, but their tastes were so vastly different it had been a futile attempt. Todd wouldn't tell Kelsey how long the affair had been going on, but it made her stomach hurt to think that it might have already been going strong that day.

Evan never talked about her.

"You wanna play?" he asked, a spark of mischief lighting his eyes. It broke through the somberness that was threatening to drag her down.

"Truth or dare? Are you serious?"

"Why not?" He reached over and lightly pinched her bare arm. She shivered.

"Aren't we a little too old for that?"

"Weren't we then? You're only as old as you act. Come on. Truth or dare?"

She grinned. "Truth." She wasn't much of a dare person. He knew that, damn him.

"All right. You were on a pre-law track with me in college. But you didn't go on to law school. You once told me you lost interest, yet you work for an attorney. So what's the story?"

Well, that was quick enough that he'd been stewing over it for a while, she decided. For a moment, she chewed a fingernail, gaze cast downward to the tabletop. She could feel him watching her. His hands were in her field of vision, resting there on the table, and she momentarily got caught up in studying them, imagining all the naughty things they could do to her. Beautiful, beautiful hands, strong and long-fingered. She'd felt their touch many times, but never in the way she fantasized about the most.

He's waiting, dummy! Did you ever have a thought that didn't involve getting him naked?

She snapped back to attention, looking at him and schooling her expression. "I was…talked out of pursuing a law degree." Given a flat-out *no* was more like it.

A line appeared between his black brows. "It's never too late."

"Right. And how do you propose I support myself for three years while I go to school? It could be done, but it would involve sacrifices I'm not willing to make right now. Like moving back home to my parents and listening to them ask me every day when I'm going to forget this nonsense and go back to being 'a *good* wife' to Todd."

"I'm sorry."

She shrugged off the gnawing regret that plagued her whenever she thought about it. "I wanted to do family law. Just from what I've seen working for Jack, I don't think I could ever do criminal—too much grit and violence and pain. I really admire you for facing the dark side like that. I just want to fight for people who are in my situation and worse. People with kids. I know I could make it, if I had the chance."

"I know you could, too. And you're right, I think it would be perfect for you. What I do, yeah, sometimes it is hard to leave it all at the office when I go home at night. Still, there's nothing like giving someone a chance to get on the stand and face down the person who hurt them." He was twirling his empty margarita glass, his gaze fixed and intent on some distant point. "To see their strength shining through. It's really incredible."

"I only have to watch you do the job to know you feel that way. And I have no one to blame but myself for letting

Todd hold me back."

"I'm sure you made what you thought was the best decision at the time. You should really keep thinking about a way to do it, though, Kels. Yes, it's three years of sacrifice, and you'll start to think you must be a masochist for putting yourself through it. But it'll go by before you know it. I know my dear friend Jack probably isn't paying you near what you're worth."

"I can make it on what I earn," she protested. "He's good to me. He did my divorce pro bono. Todd and I didn't have much to fight over, really. We sold the house, but we didn't have much equity. I took my stuff and he took his."

"At least Jack helped you out on that. He'd deserve a beat-down otherwise. Anyway, what you're doing, it's good experience. You could still do so much more, though."

She was touched he seemed so passionate about her future, but his green eyes were burning too intently at her. "Okay, enough of that," she declared. "Evan Ross, truth or dare?"

The wicked grin that spread across his face was maddening. "Dare."

Oh, he would. She had him go up to a hot blonde who'd been eyeing him ever since their arrival and act like he could only speak Italian. It probably wasn't a good idea to put him in proximity with a woman dripping diamonds and sex appeal, but it was all she could think of. What made it doubly hilarious was the slinky blonde's obvious desperation to communicate with him.

"I think you could've nailed her despite the language barrier," Kelsey laughed after he returned to their table.

"I kept waiting for you to come to my rescue, but you didn't, so now you must pay." He pointed at her. "Truth or dare? And stop being a weenie, because you never take dares."

"You never take truths. And I guess I just like revealing

things to you." She shifted in her seat as his expression slackened into one she'd have called desire if it had been on anyone else. It sent a surge of boldness through her blood. "All right, then. *Both*," she declared, and he grinned.

"Well, well. Okay. First you have to tell me something about you there's no way I could know. Shock me."

"Shock you *how*?"

"That's up to you." But his low, sexy tone of voice told her just exactly the kind of *shocking* he meant. It sent warm currents to all the right places even as she felt the blood rising in her face.

Lifting her gaze to his, she took a breath and inhaled half the margarita the waitress had just set in front of her. Evan laughed at her, one corner of his mouth turned up.

She winced as the icy slush burned down her throat, vanishing into the warmth that flowed through her veins. It was enough to loosen her inhibitions, her tongue. She ran her gaze hungrily over Evan, gorgeous specimen that he was. Good God. She'd love to loosen her tongue over him. The heat was pooling in places that had her squirming. It was like a magnet tugging her between her legs and in her breasts, pulling her straight toward him, toward the inevitable. Leaning over the table, she propped her chin in her hand.

"I've never had a vaginal orgasm." *And that's something I would love very much for you to help me out with*, she added silently. At least she hoped it was silent.

Evan's head snapped back as if her words had physically smacked him in the face. His eyebrows were practically in his hairline, his green eyes enormous. But his surprise was gone as quickly as it had manifested, and he leaned toward her, so that their noses were only a few inches apart. "*Really*."

"Did I do good? Is that the kind of shocking you had in mind?"

"That's it, pretty much, but a damn *shame*, is what that is."

He gaped at her for a moment. "Are you drunk?"

"No. I'm fine, really. Why?"

"Because you—I mean, I expected you to turn me down cold on that one. You hardly talk like that unless... Look, you have me stuttering now."

She laughed, reveling in the sense of accomplishment. She'd made Evan Ross stutter.

But he was going on. She'd dug her hole, now she had to wallow in it. "Never?"

"I just don't think I can do it," she told him with exaggerated eyelash-fluttering coquettishness. "Lots of women can't, though." She knew she was going to want to kick herself in the morning when she remembered this conversation.

"Oh, I bet you can," he said with a knowingness that curled her toes in shoes that didn't allow for much toe curling. Lisa would definitely call them medieval torture devices. "And now for your dare."

Her breath stilled. His gaze flickered down to her lips, and she parted them involuntarily. God, if he ever kissed her, she didn't know if she would be able to handle it. Once at a frat party he and some long-forgotten girlfriend had found a dark corner and made out just across the room from her. Seeing it had been as fun as a kick in the gut, but she hadn't been able to tear her gaze away from the slow, tender insistence of his mouth and the restless wandering of his hands on the girl's body. They'd finally gone up to his room. Kelsey had gone back to her dorm and cried herself to sleep. She bet those lips were just on the soft side of firm. She bet those hands would know just where to go to have her as limp and panting as that girl had been.

"Get in the pool with me."

Her brows drew together. "Okaaay. Well, that's not too..." She trailed off when she thought of the time. "Ah. It's closed by now."

"Closed and dark. But I think we need to cool off after that revelation, don't you?"

"We do have the Pacific Ocean in its entirety for that, right in our backyard. I thought you were a law-and-order guy."

"I'm on vacation. And I have an irrational fear of getting eaten alive by sharks in the inky blackness. Didn't you see *Open Water*? It's the bane of my existence."

"I didn't mean we were going miles offshore."

"It doesn't matter. They come inshore at night to feed."

"That would have been a most excellent dare for you. 'Hey, Ev, swim out a hundred yards or so and give that great white a nibble of your crunchy Italian goodness.'" She laughed as he rubbed the corner of his eye with his middle finger. "Just kidding." Despite her feigned lightheartedness, her blood was pounding feverishly through her veins. "Okay. Let's go do it."

Chapter Five

When they left the bar, she turned toward the elevator, thinking they would go up and change into their swimsuits. But Evan grabbed her hand and pulled her in the direction of the door that led to the pool area.

It was dark out there. No fence. Apparently security at such a reputable establishment didn't expect to have their patrons engage in acts of mischief. When Kelsey, in a moment of terrible uncertainty, noticed that the adjacent octagonal-shaped building that housed the hot tub was wide open, she tapped Evan on the shoulder and pointed at it. At least they would be somewhat hidden there, and someone had left the hot tub on. She could hear it. Evan grabbed her again and tugged her toward it.

"This is crazy," she whispered, her heart in her throat.

"It's okay. Trust me."

"I said I'd get in, but I didn't say how long. Just in and out, okay? Long enough to complete my dare."

He snickered. "And Brian says *I'm* too cautious."

This wasn't like him at all. He'd probably bribed someone.

It was the only thought she could take any comfort in, and probably the only way she could go through with this.

Her heart nearly pushed the rest of its way into her throat when he started unbuttoning his shirt. She cast a glance around, noticing a couple strolling toward the beach off to their right. They were at least far enough away from the main walkway that no one should even glance in their direction. And it *was* dark here in the little glass-walled building, where the ceiling shadowed them from the soft yellow glow of the security lights.

"Ugh, we're gonna get caught," she whispered, flinging off her blouse in a burst of wildness. She was too worried about someone else seeing her in her bra to be worried about Evan seeing her. Besides, she'd been strutting around in front of him in that floss Lisa had insisted she buy. Her underwear covered more than that thing. "We're gonna get caught and we're gonna get kicked out. We'll be homeless. Homeless in Hawaii."

"Not if you hurry and get in the damn water." There was laughter in his hissed words. He was stripping off his pants. Hmm, she'd always wondered whether it was boxers or briefs for him, and...ah, he wore boxer briefs. She chewed her bottom lip. The man had hands down the best ass she'd ever seen, and the sight of it accentuated by the snug material had her hands quivering as she fought with the button on her own pants. His bulge in the front did little to restore her composure; it sent her senses into a tailspin.

His movements all but silent, he eased down into the roiling water and she followed close behind, keeping a safe distance between them as the heat saturated her bones. If he touched her, she was going to embarrass herself. Moments passed while she lost herself to the bliss of the jet blowing against her lower back.

"I wish I'd never introduced you to him."

The statement was jarring in its suddenness, and weighty, as if it had been a burden bearing down on him for some time now. He avoided her gaze as he went on. "I don't know why he wanted to come visit me at school in the first place. He never had before, not in four years. I wish I'd tried to talk him out of going to that party where you met him."

"Evan, for God's sake, don't blame yourself. I cast enough blame around, on myself, on Courtney, on him…and we're all three guilty of something. But not you. If there's one truly innocent party in all this, I imagine it's you."

He shook his head, and she didn't think she'd ever seen him look so distant and forlorn. "You don't even know."

What could he have done? Something told her—and that *something* was ten years of knowing him—that he would confide in her in his own time, and now wasn't it. But something was eating away at him. "Well," she sighed, "we can't change it now, can we?"

"Would you?" he asked.

It was a question she'd pondered herself, but had never come up with a definite answer. In the end, it didn't matter. "Some days, yes. Some days, no. On one hand, it showed me what I want and don't want in a relationship, but on the other, I wish I could have avoided the whole ugly mess by whatever means necessary."

"I deal with people every day who tell me they never thought anything bad would ever happen to them. But it's not their fault that it did. You gave it your best shot."

"Sometimes I think I could have done more."

"I don't know what. When I would go over to your house and watch how you were, I was always—I always wished I could find someone like you."

She had to laugh. "Courtney was nothing like me."

"Trust me, there isn't another you."

It was said lightly but there was an undercurrent of

despair in the words. She watched the water bubble and swirl and lifted her feet so it could tickle her toes. Evan's gaze was on her. It had a familiar weight she could detect even when she wasn't looking at him.

"So why do you think you can't come during sex?"

If she'd been drinking something, she'd have spit it through her nose. Her heart was hanging by threads somewhere around her stomach at the intimacy and bluntness—he'd never said anything like that to her in all the years she'd known him. Now she was the one stuttering. Damn him. "I-I…just never…"

"He couldn't get you hot?"

Oh. My. God. Was *he* drunk? Was she? What universe was this? And he wouldn't look away from her. His gaze was inescapable. And burning. Her nerve endings came to life, agitated by the rushing water, the heat of it. Of him, so close to her. Evan Ross made her hotter just by *existing* than Todd Jacobs had in eight years of sex. All put together. It was horrible to admit.

"Evan…"

"God, Kelsey, you're looking at me like you used to."

"Huh?"

"Nothing. You haven't answered my questions."

"I can't…"

"Can't what?"

"I can't talk about this with you. I know I started it, back in the bar, but…"

His lids fell over his eyes, hooding them. She didn't know how she was supposedly looking at him, but he was looking at her as if he wanted to eat her. She couldn't be mistaking it. "He didn't take care of you," he murmured, and her breath stilled as his hand smoothed back a strand of hair plastered to her forehead. "I was afraid he wouldn't."

"Why didn't you tell me this back then?"

"I did. You didn't listen."

No, she didn't. He was right. She'd thought he was being a jerk for never wanting her yet questioning the happiness she'd finally attained with someone else. What was she supposed to do? She couldn't have Evan, yet she couldn't have anyone else, either? "I needed someone."

"You didn't *need* anyone."

"I didn't *need* anyone, but I wanted someone. And he was a good guy, for the most part. He shouldn't have done what he did, but I stopped making him happy."

He sighed. "How long ago did he stop making *you* happy?"

The question caused her to freeze. He went on. "Todd and I grew up together, lived on the same street, played baseball all through school together. I probably know him better than anyone, better than you, better even than his own parents. I've known him practically my whole life, and I'd seen him do some shady stuff before. I never thought he was quite good enough for you, but I never thought he would betray either of us like he did. Kelsey, truth be known, I don't think there's a guy walking this planet I would trust with you. So you can't really listen to me, I don't guess."

Now she could feel her blood heating and it had nothing to do with the water or his proximity. She wasn't going to condemn herself to a life of loneliness and remain a slave to this infatuation, just so Evan Ross could know she wasn't with some guy who was neglecting her needs. It made no sense. It was pissing her off.

She made a move to stand, though she had no idea where she might go. The suite keycard was in his pants—probably the only thing she would ever get out of that particular article of clothing, and that was damn fine with her at the moment—but if she ran back there he would only follow.

"Kelsey." His hand caught her arm, keeping her seated. "Don't get upset. We don't have to talk about any of this, if you don't want. But maybe it's not such a good idea to keep it bottled up."

"Then why don't you talk about Courtney? You haven't mentioned her at all."

Even in the darkness, she saw his expression tighten. "I have nothing to say about her."

"I think it hurt you more than you let on."

"Kelsey, you have to let it go. Courtney is what she is and she's not for me. Good enough? I think you need to face what happened and move on."

"Oh, I did face it, Evan Ross. I faced it head on. When I faced it, she was on top of my husband. You didn't have to see it. I did."

Kelsey sensed his demeanor change—he stiffened as if she'd doused him with ice water. "If I didn't know better, I would think you *are* blaming me for not being able to hold on to my woman." His voice had taken on a dangerous edge she'd never heard before.

She licked her lips, the urge to challenge him rising up in nearly undeniable waves. Despite her earlier words to the contrary, the thought had crossed her mind. Not lately, of course, but back when her heart had been lying in bloody shards along with her life, after having to move out of the house she loved so much into a closet-sized apartment— putting most of her stuff into storage because it wouldn't fit there and spending Christmas in Lisa and Daniel's empty house rather than facing the pity in her family's eyes—she had wondered why Evan hadn't kept Courtney happy enough to keep her hands off Todd.

But she'd been thinking irrationally. She'd made some mistakes, but she'd done everything she knew how to make her marriage work. There was no reason to believe Evan hadn't done the same with his relationship. "No, that isn't what I'm saying at all. If it were, it would go for me, too, not being able to hold on to him."

He relaxed a bit, taking his hand from her arm, but the darkness still shadowed his expression. She didn't like it there. She wanted to wipe it away. From him, from her. God, why did this have to happen to them? Adding another layer of complication over the catastrophe of their friendship?

She might as well add yet another.

"No."

A vertical line formed between his dark brows. "No what?"

"He really couldn't get me that hot. For most of our relationship, I overlooked it."

One corner of his mouth tugged upward, showing a flash of white teeth in the darkness. "Why?"

She shrugged, dropping her gaze from his. She put a hand in front of one of the water jets, letting the pressure tickle her palm. "Why did I overlook it? Because I loved him."

"Then what was missing?"

It was a good question. "I really don't know. But there was an emptiness there. Even if he got me off some other way, something was just…lacking. I never felt it as strongly as I did after we had sex."

She wasn't looking at him—she couldn't—so she tried to tune in to him in other ways, gauging the sound of his breathing, the tension in his limbs that were somehow brushing against hers now. He seemed to be holding himself perfectly still. She dared the briefest glance upward to find his gaze riveted on her. It made her suck in a breath. It trapped her.

"Am I completely crazy?" she asked.

"Not at all."

"I can't believe I'm telling you this."

"I'm glad you are. I get to be the one to assure you that you're not the problem."

She laughed, though the insinuation had her heart

brimming with hope she probably had no right to feel. "How can *you* be so sure?"

"Look at you. Beautiful, sweet. I remember how whenever I touched you your muscles would pull tight, your breath would catch. It still does. I see how you're looking at me. There's no reason a woman as sensitive and loving as you should feel *empty* after a man makes love to her. If there's a problem, it's not with you, and I get the feeling he tried to tell you it was."

Kelsey was trying to control her breathing and her pulse. Both threatened to spiral out of control at his words. Jesus Christ, he knew, he always had. And he was moving closer to her. Her eyes closed, purely an involuntary action. Her senses were overloading and one of them had to go. "Not in so many words, but yes."

"Kelsey," he whispered, his voice tinged with sweetness and reassurance, but not pity. She couldn't stand that, and he knew it. His fingers whispered across her shoulder. True to his words, her entire body pulled taut. "Come here."

She exhaled shakily and went into his arms. His chest was sleek and wet beneath her cheek, but even so, she could smell the spice of his cologne, the scent that was distinctly his. His chin settled on top of her hair. She didn't embrace him back, just curled up there in the protective circle of his comfort and tried to rest. Her mind still roiled with the agony of this nearness she couldn't do a damn thing with.

There wouldn't be any emptiness with him. She knew it. Todd might have convinced her she was the problem, but that was before she felt *this*. Even her feelings for Evan ten years ago had been immature compared to the soul-burning lust that had filled her in the past few days.

Her breasts were flattened against his chest and her nipples peaked against him, the only barrier between their flesh the thin silk of her bra. One of his hands was resting low on her back, his fingers stroking her with feathery caresses. She could swear that hand was inching downward. So slowly as to hope she wouldn't notice, or simply wouldn't say anything.

A moment later, she was certain of it. *Yes. Oh, God.* Yes. Her pussy clenched so hard she sank her teeth into her lip and cuddled closer into Evan's embrace. It was all she could do to bite down on the moan gathering in her throat. Her mouth ran dry. His breath was dragging through his chest, the rise and fall beneath her cheek becoming more pronounced.

Lifting her head, she looked up into his eyes, pouring all the invitation into her gaze that she knew how. *Please, please.*

He froze, too, staring down at her. His perfectly shaped lips parted as his gaze dropped to her mouth, and when his fingers kneaded her flesh almost imperceptibly, she sighed.

It seemed all the encouragement he needed. There in the darkness, with the only sounds the distant whisper of waves and the water lapping gently against their bodies, his lips sought hers, capturing them in the warm, soft trap of his own.

She closed her eyes, a whimper escaping her as her arms stole around his neck. He paused as if savoring that first touch, and she absorbed the shudder that went through him. He slanted his mouth over hers as the water temp rose twenty more degrees and seemed to drain all strength from her limbs.

It seemed an eternity before his hand finally cupped the curve of her ass and she was incinerated utterly, the ache that had been pooling between her legs ever since the bar flaring into a four-alarm emergency. She wanted that hand in other places. She was one ounce of self-control away from shifting to try to coax it where she needed it most.

His fingertips drew back a few inches and slid just beneath the leg of her panties. She pressed closer and opened her mouth against his, inviting the invasion of his tongue. When it slipped past her lips into her mouth, her spinning senses overloaded again and she pulled back.

"I don't know if… I mean is this…" her lips were trembling so hard she could barely move them, "…okay?"

"Why wouldn't it be?" he whispered, sounding dark, fierce.

Because we'll never be the same. I'll never be the same. Helplessly, she raised her gaze to his. She felt torn in two, dying to have him and afraid she would die if she did. She'd been a married woman for almost five years and he made her feel like a blushing virgin. "We're friends."

"So we are." He dipped down, skimming her lips with his. "Tell me you've never thought about this before. Say you don't want me, don't want this, and I'll stop."

She went boneless, knowing she couldn't lie to him. She didn't want to, not about this. The words burst out on their own. "I do. I want you. But—"

Evan barely let that note of pleading leave her before he claimed her mouth fully, putting to rest all further protests.

Oh, God. She'd hugged him countless times, planted plenty of kisses on his cheek, all chaste. There was nothing chaste now about the slow burn of his lips across hers, nothing platonic about the erotic fervor that had her breath rasping through her lungs and her thighs shaking with the need throbbing at their apex. She wanted to cry out in frustration when he moved his hand from her bottom, only to sigh when he brushed her right breast with the back of his knuckles. Her nipple tightened further, pushing against the silk barring it from his long-awaited touch. His other hand moved up into her hair, cupping her nape as his kiss turned ravenous.

He moved in front of her and the motion pressed her back into the rough concrete edge of the hot tub. She couldn't be bothered to complain. Her bra strap slipped from her shoulder with a slow slide of his fingers, baring one breast, and his kiss was tearing her heart out. He was between her legs, and his erection pressed hard against her mound.

God help her, she wanted to cover herself when he pulled back to look at her, until she heard the sound he made as his gaze caressed the skin he'd revealed. It was half moan, half growl, and it lit her blood as he filled his palms with the weight of her breasts. His cock rubbed against her clit until she thought she would launch into the stars right there. A couple of oh-so-easy adjustments and he could be inside her. Finally inside her. This was getting out of control. She was.

"Evan," she whispered against him, "not here."

"I know," he murmured, and he pulled away, licking his lips as if to collect the taste of her from them.

She expected him to stand, to lead her out of the tub. She was surprised when he put his hands on her waist and maneuvered behind her, turning her until she faced away from him. "What are you doing?"

"Giving you no more time to think," he murmured with wicked mischief, his lips grazing her ear. His hand slid down her wet thigh to her knee, lifting it out of the water and placing her foot on the seat of the hot tub. "Just a few more minutes." Her heart nearly leapt out of her throat as the water gushing from one of the jets swirled right over her clit. A full body shudder went through her and she sobbed.

"Too much?" he asked silkily, his voice a deep rumble at her back.

"N-no. It's perfect."

He left his hand there on the inside of her thigh, stroking and soothing, while the other hand cupped her breast. His fingertips played over her peaked nipple. She wanted to jump up and run away, to flee from this power that threatened to swamp her, but she needed to have this, would suffer any humiliation for it. She could feel something incredible building from the relentless vibrating pressure of the water but she craved his fingers inside her, wanted him inside her.

Her need finally drove the words out. "Evan, please,

touch me."

He uttered a low growl, and his fingers slid between her inner thigh and the edge of her panties. She almost came on the spot. *Not yet, oh, not yet.*

He moaned her name when his roaming hand discovered she was smooth and bare there, and he slid his feverish mouth along her neck. He shifted behind her so that the ridge of his erection nudged the crease of her bottom. She bit down on her lip as he parted her folds and pushed one finger deep inside her, then a second, stretching her until she ached to cry out.

And two things happened. A door opened across the walkway—not really near them, but not at a safe distance by any means. And her orgasm slammed into her and she arched back against him, desperately holding in her cries, raising her hands to clutch his arms.

His fingers and the water worked her into a frenzy, and his other hand moved from her breast to her mouth, covering it gently, his finger slipping horizontally between her lips. She sank her teeth into his flesh, riding the pleasure in utter silence when she wanted to scream it at the moon. It wasn't the shivery pulses she was accustomed to—she'd been driven head-on into a brick wall of ecstasy, and it was crashing down over her. One whimper escaped her, and his lips grazed her left ear.

"Shhhh." The sound was so soft and erotic her pussy clenched on his fingers buried inside her. He pushed them deeper in response.

Someone emerged from the door and headed away from them as she fell limp and safe against him, panting, her heart beating like a hummingbird's wing. He was rock hard against the soft flesh of her ass and, oh, he felt enormous. She reached behind her to investigate him, and her breath caught on a groan. "Oh my God."

He chuckled, moving his hand from her lips over her chin and down her throat, caressing her breast again. "That's music to a man's ears." Gently he withdrew his fingers from between her legs, and she felt him lift his head and throw a quick glance around. "Now I think we'd better take this into the suite," he whispered.

"I don't think I can walk just yet."

"Then I'll carry you."

How, how, *how* had that stupid woman let this man go? For *Todd*?

They lingered a few moments more, Evan stroking and petting her, running his lips along her neck, her shoulder. She was horrified when she felt tears well up, but thankfully she was wet all over, so he didn't have to know when she lost the battle and they slipped over her cheeks.

He helped her from the hot tub and they struggled back into their clothes, a difficult task on their wet flesh. They simply carried their shoes. Hot tears kept dripping off her chin, and she knew she'd better get a grip. God knew this was too perfect to ruin, and they still had all night ahead.

"Are you all right?" he asked. "My offer to carry you still stands." He winked at her.

"I'm fine." She was horrified at the strangle in the words. She wasn't fine, and she knew it. This hadn't happened in months, this knot of emotion swelling in her chest until she thought it would tear out of her body and destroy everything in its path.

Only it wasn't anger this time. Not anger, but...it was the hurt. The carelessness with which her heart had been stomped underfoot. Sometimes it surged up and she couldn't contain it. But why *now*? Must be the tequila, she thought, coupled with the mind-shattering orgasm jarring all this loose. And the fact that she wanted so much more of him.

Evan held her hand all the way to their suite, absorbing

quivers she tried to pretend were from the chill of the air conditioning. She stood dripping and shuddering and silently weeping in the hallway while he unlocked their door and pushed it open for her. Head ducked, she rushed past him into the room, hoping he wasn't watching her too closely.

She should have known better. He dropped his shoes and shut the door, moving to stand behind her. A moment later one of his hands slid over her shoulder. The other reached around to pry her shoes from her death grip and toss them away. "Kelsey."

The gentleness in his voice broke her. She whirled around, folding herself into the circle his arms made around her. He caught her, strong and solid, crushing her to him as she sobbed into his damp shirt. She heard his long sigh rush through his airways.

"Get rid of it, sweetheart," he murmured, stroking her hair. "Give it to me. All of it."

She couldn't believe the words that were rising in her throat, demanding to be spoken, but there was no help for them. She was on the verge of having something that had been well beyond her reach for so many years, something she'd never thought she'd have. He couldn't deny her now. She couldn't deny herself. "I need you."

"Tell me."

She raised her burning, blurred gaze to his. The voice that sounded from her throat couldn't have been her own. "I need you to fuck me, Evan, fuck me until I can't walk anymore. I don't care if you hurt me, just do it."

"*Goddammit*," he rasped, and she'd never heard him sound so savage. His hands seized her head, tilting her face upward, and his kiss chased the breath from her lungs. She made some wild animal snarl in her throat and grasped his hair, ready to climb him like a tree if it would get his cock inside her any faster.

His arm swept down under her ass and lifted her. She clung haphazardly as he carried her into the bedroom, not wanting to let go even when he tossed her back on the bed. She writhed, rubbing her thighs together, watching him stare down at her for what seemed an endless moment. He was completely silhouetted in the light from the living room, but she imagined he could see her well enough. It wasn't fair.

"What?" she demanded.

"Nothing."

She'd never wanted to be naked more in her entire life, and she couldn't wait on him to get her that way. When she sat up to strip her slinky blouse off over her head, he grabbed it first and gave it a fling across the room. It was a struggle to kick off her clinging pants, and he had to help her with that, too, freeing her bare legs from the damp material.

All strength fled then in the aching rush that flooded her and she collapsed on the mattress, trying to wrestle back control of her breathing. He crawled over her and hooked his fingers in her panties. His eyes caught a glint of the dim light as he stripped the delicate fabric down her bare legs, nearly ripping it.

Oh, *Jesus*, was this happening? She'd had this dream so many times in the past month, sometimes so vivid she could swear it was real until she woke in her bed sweating and aching and alone. But this Evan wasn't going to disappear into the darkness of her bedroom. This was real.

"My God," he murmured, and she covered her face with her hands and sobbed in pleasure and mortification as he caught the back of her knee in one hand and pushed her legs open so wide her muscles trembled. "I just have to," he whispered, then he dipped his dark head, and the soft, damp warmth of his mouth covered her. His tongue lined her, licked deeper at her moisture, flickered over her clit.

Panic ripped through her and the room spun. She pulled

her hands away to make a grab for his hair, but on direct orders from her heart, twisted the bed's comforter in her fists instead. *Let him! Oh, God, let him.*

She thought she would die from the warmth of his breath on her burning flesh. It was almost a relief when he kissed and licked a trail up her belly, keeping her legs held open wide. He paused to circle her belly ring with his tongue then to nuzzle the silk of her bra and lock his lips around each nipple in turn through the fabric on his pathway up to her mouth.

She absorbed his weight greedily and feasted on his lips. He tasted of tangy margaritas and *her*, so slick and delicious. He tugged her upward long enough to relieve her of her soggy bra, which hit the wall with a wet slap. She fumbled with the button on his pants, but her hands were shaking violently against his taut stomach muscles and her fingers felt thick, much like the rest of her body. Evan's hands joined hers, steady and sure and urgent, tugging and pushing until a moment later his rigid length sprang into her hand.

Kelsey stroked the steely silken smoothness of him, and he uttered a gruff sound that evoked a purely feminine response from her own lips. He was big. She'd known that from touching him before. Her eyes had adjusted and the little light there was showed her he was beautiful, as she'd also known he would be. She looked down to watch her hand smooth over his cock, her thumb rubbing the slit in the head, collecting the pearl of liquid that had formed there. He let her play, his breathing labored, until she felt his fingers thrust inside her. She arched back on the bed, releasing him to clutch his biceps as he dragged his fingers from her and spread her wetness over her clit.

"Are you ready for me, baby?"

The endearment curled warmly through her senses, intimate and unfamiliar coming from him. But they were three thousand miles away from familiar. "*Yes.*" Her hands skated feverishly over his shoulders as she imagined him riding her to an ecstasy she'd never before attained. If anyone could give that to her, it was him. "But are you ready for me?"

He chuckled as his fingers slid in and out again, thickly glazed with her need. "You like throwing down challenges, don't you?"

Oh, damn him. She moaned and tossed her head on the mattress, raising one leg to brush against his side, to give him better access. "I just want you. Don't make me wait anymore. Please, Evan, now."

He released her only to seize her wrists in both his hands and slam them back on the bed, shifting above her to position himself and attacking her lips with his own. She sprawled wider for him, feeling ten pounds heavier in her lower belly, liquid with her want. The thick head of his cock teased her opening, and she squirmed, trying to force it deeper, trying to impale herself.

"Easy, sweetheart," he whispered.

"I don't want it easy. Inside me, I need you inside—"

He listened. He plunged directly into that molten center, and a shockwave pulsed through her body though she'd accepted only half his length.

"*Evan!*"

He groaned in her ear, retreating and reclaiming, going deeper until he lodged against her cervix. She struggled to accommodate him, wrapping her legs around his hips, needing all of him, the simultaneous pleasure and pain slaying her. It had been too long. Tears streamed from her eyes.

"God, Kelsey, you're killing me here."

"Don't stop, don't stop...*ohhh...*"

"No, sugar. I couldn't if I wanted to." So wet and slick and tight inside her. His long, slow slides in and out of her body set off sparks, like Fourth of July fireworks grazing her flesh.

She was nearly hyperventilating. "Faster."

"Oh, yes," he groaned, his voice shaking. His fingers twined through hers, still pinning her hands in place, and he set a merciless rhythm that drove her into the stratosphere. Her pussy adjusted to the overwhelming stretch and accepted him greedily. The silence of the bedroom was broken by the wet sounds of their joining and their rapid breathing, and she found herself drawing as much excitement from his pleasure as her own.

"I want to touch you—" she sobbed.

"Only after I make you come so hard you scream my name. And you will." That purred oath alone nearly drove her over. It was the same voice that had made her spew coffee at her office two weeks ago, so deep and seductive, like dusky velvet. "You scream it as loud as you want this time."

Her tears were still flowing in earnest. He smeared the trail with his lips, his breath warm and panting against her cheek. She had asked for this, and he was giving it to her, but terror churned through her middle. The sparks were igniting. She didn't know what would be left of her heart once the explosion was over.

Every inch of her was alive in a way she couldn't recall ever having experienced. She'd never been so enflamed, so wet. She loved how he felt inside her, thick and overpowering. The swaying of her breasts as he pushed into her again and again was almost like a physical caress to their aching weight. She arched upward so her nipples would graze his dark smattering of chest hair. But when he raised his head to look at her, she had to turn away—his regard for her was too intense, too powerful.

"Kelsey." He whispered her name so sweetly she whimpered. "You're perfect. Don't close up on me now, sweetheart, let me see you."

She turned her head back to find him staring down into her eyes. The expression she saw there made her heart trip over itself. He looked at her as if he were trying to get inside her soul as surely as he was inside her body. She knew her own gaze was simply desperate, pleading.

Like building thunderheads in the distance, she could feel it gathering, the towering pressure tightening deep inside her womb until she could hardly stand it... *please please please...*

"Evan...oh *God...*"

"Just let it go," he murmured, watching the fragmented emotions she knew were crossing her face. "It's going to be so good."

Oh, it was. His lips grazed hers as all hell broke loose in her body and she surrendered to it—that's all she could do. One small part of her pulled her entire body taut as ecstasy burst outward from the heavy thrust and drag where he claimed her. She clenched down on him, crying out his name. True to his promise.

"There you go, baby. *Christ.*"

He buried himself more fully inside her and sharpened his movements, driving her through it, and the sobs lodged in her throat broke out in staccato bursts when she couldn't draw enough breath to scream. Her hands gripped his hard enough to snap bones. She tossed her head back and forth, the only part of her she still maintained control of. She was his, every inch, held open and immobile, captive to her passion for him. Like wind gusts during a hot summer storm, it swept her away.

"Fuck, honey, do I need to pull out? You feel too good."

"No, no, don't leave me, it's okay." She locked her legs tighter around him and held on as her final contractions milked him of all restraint. His hips slammed forward and he surged inside her, pulsing with his release. He said her name, growled it, as she drank in the sight of him, the sensation of him spilling himself inside her. So thick and warm. His hair fell forward around his face and the veins stood out in his neck. God, he was exquisite.

One final thrust and he eased himself down over her, his chest heaving. His hand smoothed up her arm and he palmed her breast, turning his face into her neck. With her hands finally free, she wrapped her arms around him and held on as if he were a life preserver. He felt different from her ex, leaner, all sinewy strength and coiled power. He took better care of himself. Did everything better.

She was shaking like a palm frond in a hurricane, unable to stop the helpless little sounds that kept slipping through her lips. With complete concentration she managed one deep, cleansing breath to coax down her ragged pulse. The scent of their sex bloomed throughout the room, filling her nostrils. Now that the heat they'd generated had rushed out of her, she could feel the blush roaring high and hot in her cheeks.

No, no, don't leave me…

She cringed, digging her fingertips into his flesh as an anchor against the surge of embarrassment that heated her blood, so different from the intoxicating fires of moments ago. Jesus, what had she done? "Oh, God," she whispered, covering her face with one hand.

"It's okay, Kelsey."

"No, it…" She couldn't speak. He pulled himself from her, then snuggled close and brought her into his embrace.

"Sweetie. Look at me."

She did, but it was difficult now, when she could never remember a time she hadn't wanted to look at his beloved face. She blinked, trying to force the fresh torrent of tears back where they belonged. It just wasn't possible.

No, there was no emptiness now. She was bursting at the seams, overflowing.

"Don't cry," he said gently, swiping her cheeks with his thumbs. "You cry and I want to break something. Or someone. What is it?"

"I can't. I'm sorry. Not right now."

All this time…all these years. All her restless longing had converged on her at once.

"Okay, okay." His eyes were troubled as he stroked her hair. "Just answer me this. Do you regret it?"

She hated that she was making him look like that, but there was nothing she could do except reply to that question truthfully, and without hesitation. "No. Don't ever think that. And I'm okay, really." She drew a deep breath and felt the panic start to pass. They were both adults, they would be all right. It was rather late for the protection discussion, but she felt the need to ease his mind. "I'm on the Pill, so you don't have to worry."

He chuckled, his warm breath tickling her cheek. "I'm really not worried, honey."

Okay. She stroked her fingertips up and down his spine as long minutes passed and she puzzled over that. The image that flashed through her mind then was unavoidable: a dark-haired toddler smiling up at her with Evan's green eyes. What unsettled her most was that it only made her want to maul him again.

You only had sex with the guy. Stop thinking about white picket fences, dammit. It was almost as if she could hear Lisa's voice in her mind, chiding her.

So she did what it commanded. Amazing, to just let go and drift on this euphoria. To finally hold him in the carnal embrace she'd fantasized about for so long.

Chapter Six

Evan watched Kelsey struggle bravely with her tears. He only wished he knew what to say to help her win the battle with them, but what was there to say when your best friend was weeping with guilt over finally having mind-blowing sex with you?

Goddammit. There was so much he wanted to tell her, but to do so now might shatter her fragile calm. Still, he marveled at her dramatic shift from wounded kitten to hellcat and back again, and wanted to break Todd Jacobs's freaking neck for hurting her. She should have let him do it seven months ago when he'd tried.

Because that's what this was about, wasn't it? Her anger, her hurt, her betrayal. All taken out on him.

It was all right. Hell. He could take it, and consider himself a lucky guy for it.

"Mmm, I don't want to let you go," he murmured in her ear finally. "So sweet and warm."

She sighed, running the sole of one foot up and down his calf. His body stirred at the gesture, thinking of those perfect feet, pretty and dainty with little seashell toenails. Everything about her body was pretty and dainty.

"We can sleep like this," she suggested, smiling dreamily at him. They were still wrapped tight in each other's arms. She was heavenly soft against him.

"We will. But I'm not ready to sleep just yet." He made the words as rich with erotic promise as he knew how. Guilt or no, she couldn't deny that it had been good. It had been very, very good. They couldn't unring a bell. Might as well ring it again.

"Really?" she asked, a tinge of amazement in her voice, in those reawakened gray eyes as she looked at him.

He supposed that meant his former best friend had been down for the count after one shot. "You'd better believe it." He grinned, bringing her hand down to wrap around his thickening cock. "Because I think you're still capable of walking right now."

The peace that had settled over her expression shattered in anguish. He put his fingers to her lips as she opened her mouth, undoubtedly to wail in mortification. "Honey, that was the hottest thing that's ever been said to me, and you're going to stop being embarrassed about what you want, if I'm the one who has to break you of it. Nothing we do together is wrong, especially after what was done to us."

She closed her eyes and her trembling started all over again—he took it as permission. Thank God. Once more, even if it was the last time.

He spent a good amount of time exploring the silken skin that had too often been so close to him, yet so far away. She'd trusted him with her body, and he cherished every square inch of it with his touch, his lips, but he had to keep coming back to her breasts. They were lovely; they fit his hands perfectly. He slid his mouth down over her flesh and encircled her nipple with his lips. Warmth gathered in the skin beneath his wet ministrations, and he swirled his tongue around the sweet pearled tip before he suckled it gently. Her fingers tightened around his cock, sending a jolt through him so intense that he groaned against her.

He couldn't wait any longer. He pulled his lips away from her and shifted, bringing himself between her smooth thighs. She opened for him, her hand still stroking him. Her lips parted as she gazed up at him and he accepted the invitation, taking a mouthful of her sweetness, and then another and another.

"Put me inside you," he whispered urgently, bracing himself above her on his arms, and then nearly came right there as she gave him one loving stroke and moved the head of his dick to the swollen, scalding liquid center of her. So small and smooth, and *bare*... She had to have done that for him, just on the hope of this. He wouldn't disappoint her. He forced himself to ease inside, savoring the feel of her taut inner muscles parting before him. Every neuron in his spinal column crackled with pleasure. She was so damned tight, and wet with his come. He gave her a little and pulled back, then a little more. Until she was writhing beneath him.

"Evan," she whispered, entangling her fingers in his hair as he took her all the way and began to move through her. Kelsey started to bring her other hand up to his shoulder, but he shook his head and brought it back down between their bodies, until her fingers came into contact with his wet shaft disappearing into her flesh.

"Stay there. Feel us," he murmured. She sighed as his fingers slid through hers, both of them stroking and caressing where he ended and she began as he thrust slowly into her. He was thick and straining, damp from their combined juices. Her slick folds were parted wide to accommodate him.

"That's beautiful," she said, and moaned.

"We're good together." He managed to give her a smile,

but it most likely came out weak. *Beautiful.* She was so beautiful she broke his heart. She always had.

He pulled all the way out so she could smooth her hand over his length before he slid slowly, inexorably back in. He groaned when she caressed his sac, very gently squeezing it. She whimpered when his fingers would drag across her clit.

He could grow addicted to this, to the way she shivered around him as he fucked her. She caught his mouth with hers, sweet and tentative, and he returned her kiss reassuringly. Her tongue danced between his lips, tangling tenderly with his. He explored her mouth in turn, the softness, the wet heat, the hard edge of her teeth. Her flavor was as scrumptious as the rest of her.

"My God, Kelsey." His breathing was growing ragged, his blood racing as the tension at the base of his spine threatened to fling him into the ozone. "So good it hurts." He was so achingly hard inside her yielding softness he couldn't comprehend how he wasn't hurting her. She was moaning, a faint tremor working its way through her as he increased the urgency of his thrusts by increments. His hand abandoned the place of their joining so he could brace himself above her, so he could give her everything he had, but she kept exploring the feel of them together and it was driving him out of his skull.

"Please," she whispered. "Harder. Make me come like that again, it was so good, Evan."

"It makes me so goddamned crazy when you talk like that."

He gathered her in his arms and rolled them over so that she straddled him on top. She squeaked, and he nearly shot his load as the new position seemed to allow him to plunder new depths in her body. "Take me however you need," he told her, hearing the harshness in his own words. His hands molded to her hips then he moved them upward to cup her breasts in the curves of his thumb and index finger. Her eyes glittered down at him in the faint moonlight now spilling in from the window, but she looked unsure of herself. "Do it, baby. Let me watch you."

She squeezed her inner muscles and he flexed in response. She smiled. Then she proceeded to kill him as she pulled his hands from her breasts and pushed his wrists back on the mattress.

"You can touch me after I make you come so hard you scream my name."

"Dammit—"

She laughed, the vixen, and he was tempted to show her he could break her grip any time he wished. But she wanted control, and he wanted her to have it. The woman had no shame now as she worked his cock, and he thought of some pagan goddess as her dark hair tossed against skin turned milky by the moonlight.

He watched in agony as she sought the angle she needed and nearly died from relief when she found it and each stroke began to force a whimper from her throat. God, his abdomen muscles were cramping from holding back. Her weight was on his wrists now, and his gaze locked on the mesmerizing sight of her swaying breasts as the wet sheath between her thighs swallowed him over and over again.

The rhythm she'd struck was sensual and torturous, slower than he would've liked, but he complied with it, thrusting up to meet her. When her muscles began to clamp hard around him it took everything within him to keep from breaking her hold on him so he could rub her clit, desperate for her climax to shake loose and milk him. All he could do was curl his toes, close his eyes, hold on and pray...

"Oh, baby," she cried. "Evan, I didn't know it could feel like this..."

...but he could endure any torture if it made her cry out

words like that, if it gave her pleasure she'd never known before.

"Mmm, you're turning me inside out. I won't last much longer, honey."

The devious little smile that curled her lips nearly killed his soul. Oh, God, it was coming, welling up, and he couldn't stop it.

She arched above him just as his control broke and he shattered, erupting into her with everything she hadn't drained him of before. It tore loose from his goddamn soul. Kelsey's feminine cries were like music as her strokes up and down his shaft lengthened and sped, sucking greedily at him. He couldn't stand it. He took advantage of her weakened state to break her grip and grab her, pulling her down hard into his arms as he thrust the last of his come as deep into her quivering depths as he could push it. Her name rolled compulsively from his lips into the soft shell of her ear. Jesus. A honeysuckle-scented cloud of her hair smothered him and her softness enveloped him as the last of their tension bled into one another.

He was so through with running from her.

Silent moments passed, and Kelsey was grateful when he began to caress her, smoothing his fingers along her spine, stroking her hair. She didn't think she could have dealt with the aftermath of this raging passion between them without him soothing her, whispering endearments. Her heart felt swollen to the point of filling her chest. She feared it was about to spill out of her mouth, and God knew she didn't want to say anything to shatter this.

So she settled on what she always said when he left her aghast.

"Jesus Christ, Evan Ross."

He laughed and ran his lips over her cheek. "I knew I'd make you say it sooner or later. You do know a very hard decision is ahead of us." He paused, letting suspense build. "Sleep or shower?"

A relieved breath rushed out of her. She was too emotionally spent to consider anything deeper than that. Sleep sounded heavenly. She was exhausted and raw. But at the same time, she was coated with a fine sheen of sweat and a mingling of the remnants of their lovemaking.

"Shower," she murmured. "Quick, before I go to sleep." He slid free from her as she lifted her hips and she mourned his loss right away. Amazing that even after three earth-shattering orgasms, she could still crave him in such a way. She already couldn't wait for tomorrow.

Tomorrow.

You're thinking again, she chided herself.

They climbed out of bed and padded into the bathroom. As he turned on the water in the shower she got her first thorough look at his fully naked physique and felt her heart drop to her feet. *Damn.*

He'd been downright edible in his boxer briefs out by the hot tub, and that had been in the dark. Now she could hardly breathe. His sports had always been track and swimming, tennis and baseball, and they'd certainly leant to his trim, firm build. There wasn't an ounce of bulk on his frame, just as she liked. He could've been an underwear model, only she preferred him like this, without a stitch on.

When he stood to the side to let her enter the shower first, her gaze fell to the dark nest of hair at the juncture of his thighs. The sight made her want to hit her knees right there on the cold bathroom floor and take him into her mouth, suck him until he exploded down the back of her throat.

What else was he going to teach her about herself?

One night with him and she was climaxing vaginally and contemplating blowjobs, she thought with a wry smile. Unbelievable.

The hot spray hit her as she stepped into the shower and she nearly moaned in pleasure, ducking her head so that it ran over her hair and down the back of her neck in tickling rivulets. Evan entered behind her and reached around so he could pick up her shampoo bottle from the little shelf in front of her. After a moment, his sudsy hands sank into her hair, pulling it gently into a ponytail before piling it atop her head so he could work the lather in. She did moan when his fingers massaged her scalp. He did it for a long time, certainly longer than was necessary to clean her hair. God, but the man must love giving her pleasure. He'd given her enough tonight for a lifetime, and still she wanted more.

"Turn around, honey," he said, just as she was beginning to contemplate falling asleep while standing. She obeyed, her breasts brushing his chest as she turned. Her gaze lifted to his face while he smoothed her hair back from her forehead, making sure the water rinsed all the suds out. His expression was intent on the task, his touch raising gooseflesh despite the steamy heat billowing around them.

"Evan," she murmured, feeling that damned fullness rise in her throat again. Would she never purge it all?

He gently wrung out her hair and looked down into her face. Even through her mental turmoil a little part of her marveled at the beauty of his striated green eyes. "What is it, sweetheart?"

"It breaks my heart what they did to you, no matter how you feel about it. If Todd had to hurt me, fine, but I can't forgive him for what he did to you."

"I'm resilient, Kelsey. You don't have to worry about me."

"I know. But I didn't see you for a long time after it happened. I *was* worried about you, but I didn't think you wanted to hear from me."

"It wasn't you. That week was crazier in more ways than one. I lost what was supposed to be a slam-dunk aggravated robbery case."

Oh, God. Had it been her fault? She shouldn't have reacted the way she had, calling him like that, getting him upset in the middle of a trial. It just kept getting worse and worse. "Because of what happened. I'm so—"

"Shh. No. I'd already rested my case and the defense was thin, to say the least. It was just one of those things, I guess. And I had let it go, until the next month, when the defendant who got off *allegedly* broke into a woman's house, robbed her and raped her." His eyes darkened. "And it's my fault, because for whatever reason, I didn't do a good enough job to put him away. That crushed me more than anything Courtney could have done."

Her heart cracked again, lost another piece. How selfish she'd been. "Did they catch the guy?"

"Yeah. Of course the bastard has pled not guilty. I wanted the case, but the DA advised me to step away. Said I've made it personal now."

"Have you?"

"Of course I have. How could I not? But will that cloud my judgment or trip me up and get me flustered? Hell, no. I'm better than that. What I hate is the idea of someone arguing that case who *doesn't* make it personal." Consternation flickered across his features. "You know, you're the first person who's asked me that, instead of automatically jumping to my defense and telling me my superior is just being an ass. You're the first to not try to tell me I shouldn't feel the way I do about losing."

"Because I can understand," she said softly. "And it's *not* your fault, but I know you, you've always had a soft heart for victims. I just wish I'd known what you were going through."

"I wanted to call you more than I did, but I thought it might upset you to hear from me. I guess that was stupid of me. I also realized after what happened that I needed to work through some things on my own."

"Things were so screwed up," she agreed. "That day I saw you in court at my divorce hearing…I just wanted to die." She took a breath, knowing how awful that sounded. But she couldn't sum up the misery of that horrible day any other way. He'd been the only bright spot and even he had burned.

"I'm sorry if my being there was a trigger for you," he said, pulling her back to the present. "Just our bad luck I was the one handling pleas that day."

"No, it's all right. I was glad you were there, but…I can't explain. Ashamed that you were seeing me there, like that."

"Honey, don't ever be ashamed with me. Haven't we been through enough without that having to factor in? I've never once judged you for anything that happened."

"I know that. But my pride was hanging somewhere around my ankles that day. I don't think anyone could have rescued it."

He smiled, and though it was just a sweet curving of his lips, it was akin to the sun breaking through thunderheads. He trailed his finger down her cheek. "I always thought this, but I see now more than ever that Todd was one crazy son of a bitch for letting you go. He traded fire for ice."

He couldn't know what those words meant to her. She sighed as she agonized over what she wanted to tell him next. Absently, she picked up his bottle of body wash and squeezed some into her hands, lathered it and began soaping his chest. "I thought about it a lot, and I finally came to the decision that they needed one another because they're just alike. Careless and selfish. But…"

He waited patiently, and she was certain her touch helped him out with that, because he smiled and closed his eyes as she moved her hands over his shoulders and down both his biceps. She took just as much pleasure in the concentration of his masculine scent wafting into her nostrils.

"I have to be honest," she went on hesitantly. "Now I know...I wouldn't have married him if I'd known what I was missing out on."

She continued soaping him, and he reached for her conditioner and finished washing her hair. "He was your first," he said after a moment. It wasn't a question.

"Yes." She eyed him suspiciously. "He never told you that, did he?"

"No. I just always knew, or at least suspected. You never dated anyone, or even showed any interest in anyone, until him."

Because of you. She wondered briefly if he actually knew her better than anyone else on earth. If felt that way sometimes. Certainly no one else understood what she'd been through like he did. Not Lisa, not her family.

He moved closer, and she could only whimper as he sank into her for a warm, deep kiss that had her fearing electrocution there under the falling water. His tongue swirled with hers and her knees went rubbery. He backed her against the shower wall and she was astounded when she felt him growing hard against her abdomen. The man had stamina.

"I love how you tremble for me," he whispered. "I love how you're shy until you need me and then you aren't ashamed to tell me what you want."

I love everything about you. The thought dropped into her mind like a stone in a still pond and caused just as much disturbance. She certainly loved everything they'd done tonight. In the mornings, just the sight of him in his pajama pants checking his e-mail with his hair all mussed made her weak in the knees. She loved that he was left-handed. He chewed his thumbnail when he was engrossed in reading or watching something on TV, and she loved that, too.

He slid his hands upward to cup her breasts, his eyes flickering down toward them. "You're more beautiful than I ever imagined. And I imagined a lot."

"Y-you did?"

"Oh, yeah. It might make me a dog, mentally undressing my friend's wife, but I couldn't help myself." He sighed, and the sound made moisture that had nothing to do with the shower pool between her legs. She closed her eyes as he ran his fingertips over her nipples, peaked already from the caress of the water. "Pink," he murmured. "I always wondered, but I should have known. Soft and delicate, like the rest of you."

One of his hands trailed down to caress her clit, swollen and peeking from between her folds. She moaned, leaning her head back against the wall. Involuntarily, she lifted her foot to brace it against the side of the tub, giving him better access. Her muscles tightened as one fingertip dragged across her aching nub, back and forth, so slowly, then circled it, only to repeat the pattern. She gripped his firm, straining biceps for support when her knees started to grow weak.

"But this," he whispered against her ear, his voice almost blending with the *whoosh* of the falling water. "I had no idea you would be bare down here. God, I love it, it drives me crazy. I didn't have a chance to finish what I started. I'm going to lick you and suck you until you fly apart. You're going to open your eyes in the morning only to find yourself coming in my mouth."

Before she could dissolve into a pool of desire at his feet, she had time for one final thought: she was going to treat Lisa to a full day at the spa for saying three little words: *Shave it, girl.*

Panting, sliding down the wall, going boneless, she still gripped him. Never had she thought she could actually collapse from sensory overload. Evan caught her up in his arms, cradling her as he stepped out of the shower with her, leaving it running. "You're exhausted, sweetie."

"Mm-hmm."

"Be still, I'll take care of you."

Kelsey was only vaguely conscious of the fact that he sat her on the bed and left her to get a towel. Well, she couldn't be bothered with all that. She curled onto her side and pulled the comforter over her, flirting with the peacefulness of sleep. Until she was rudely pulled upward again to the sound of Evan's laughter, and he was stripping away her warm cover, baring her damp flesh to the air-conditioned chill, ignoring whatever incoherent protests she managed to give. A towel swept around her and another began rubbing vigorously over her hair, before he piled her damp locks on top of her head and wrapped them up. Once she was dried to his satisfaction, he picked her up easily and settled her into her spot on the bed, pulling the covers over her.

"Dream of me, sweetheart," was the last thing she heard him say before dark waves washed over her mind, finally submerging her completely.

Kelsey groaned, sleep still fogging her mind. She was aching. Between her legs. Everything felt thick and heavy and swollen and the taste of desire was flooding her mouth. Consciousness flowed in and out. Evan... She'd been dreaming about him. She still was. The pleasure he'd given her. Flashbacks had been tormenting her all night. Even now, she was thinking of her legs being spread apart, of him lowering his face to the secret place there. She was self-conscious about it—always had been—because God, it was so intimate.

Feverishly, she tossed her head. Her breasts were flooded with sensation, her nipples stiffening against nothing but air.

She was naked, not covered. Her legs were sprawled wide, and she'd never felt so open, so revealed, but damn, it was hot. Something firm and wet was flickering over the tender, throbbing nub between her thighs. She moaned, rocking her hips just a bit toward the pleasure of it, sliding one hand over a breast to tease her nipple while the other hand wandered down toward the epicenter of this sensation. So close, so close… Lips closed around her clit, and a delicious suction gripped it, so precise that starbursts exploded behind her closed eyes.

It was enough to bring Kelsey wide awake then, just in time to feel Evan slip his shoulders beneath her thighs and hold her folds open with his thumbs so he could draw her entire aching nub into the wet heat of his mouth. Sunlight flooded the room, revealing every bare inch of her to him.

There was no time for embarrassment as he suckled her again. She erupted. He thrust two fingers deep inside her pussy to feel her contractions as she pulled tight all over and grasped his silky hair with both hands, needing an anchor against the sensations buffeting her as she screamed his name again and again.

"Mmm," he murmured when she collapsed back on the bed, sated beyond all belief. But only until he crawled up the length of her body. "Good morning, angel." He moved to nudge the head of his cock teasingly against her entrance. "And he says good morning, too."

"Ohh, Evan," she moaned, shifting to take him in just slightly. Her body seemed to reach for him without her conscious thought. But she winced when he pushed, her sensitive, enflamed tissues reminding her that she'd had lots of hard sex last night after months of having none at all.

"Okay, honey?"

"I'm a little sore. He said 'Good morning' and she said 'Are you *serious*?'"

His laugh was sudden and infectious. She loved the sound of it so much. "You crack me up. Should I—*he* stop?"

"No way. She says just tell him to go slow this time, be good," she whispered.

"He is hers to command." He captured her lips with his. She could taste herself, tangy and mysterious.

Evan wrapped her in his arms, holding her close, whispering soothing words as he entered her so slowly her parting inner muscles scarcely protested him. Her extreme wetness from her orgasm eased his way.

"Baby," he groaned when his hips locked against hers. "All right? Don't let me hurt you."

She nodded, more concerned about the tightness in her throat and whether it was another dam about to burst. She opened her eyes to look up at him, determined to match him, to not turn into a simpering idiot again. "I love how we feel together," she whispered. "I don't think I could take any more, but I wouldn't want any less. It's so perfect."

He moved his hips almost imperceptibly, giving her time for her swollen passage to become reacquainted with his girth. "*Christ*," he gasped. "I feel like if I move, I'll explode."

She leaned up to his ear. "I'm going to suck you before this is over," she whispered, and dipped the tip of her tongue briefly against the soft shell. "So don't spend yourself too soon."

He seemed at a loss for a moment, groaning and leaning his forehead against hers when she lay back down. "Now," he growled. "I'd love you to suck me now. Will you?" When she nodded, he pulled out of her and she gasped at the sudden loss, the emptiness he left behind.

Oh, God, she couldn't wait to get her lips around him. He had hardly reclined against the mountain of pillows when she grasped his hips and licked up the length of him, tasting a concentration of her juices and his delectable flesh. He

groaned, reaching down to wrap her hair in his fist. He was…
oh, too gorgeous for words. She curled her hand around the
base of his cock, nestling it against the pitch black nest of
hair, and leaned forward to swirl her tongue around the head,
getting a jolt of saltiness when she swept over the milky drop
beading at the slit. She would coax more of that from him, she
vowed.

Her tongue prowled the length and girth of him while he
groaned and clutched the bedsheet in one hand and her hair
in the other. Finally, with slowness meant to agonize him, she
slid her lips over him and drew in all she could, raising her
hand up his shaft to meet her lips. He touched the back of her
throat and she softened her muscles there because it wasn't
enough, she wanted more.

"Christ you're beautiful," she heard him whisper, and
glanced up to see that he was watching through half-closed
eyes as she swallowed him and withdrew, again and again. She
imagined what she must look like to him, her hair wild from
sleep and sex cascading over his hips and thighs, her lips pink
and swollen from friction wrapped around his cock. She *felt*
beautiful in that moment. For the first time in years.

He moaned her name and turned his face up, closing his
eyes. His fist tightened in her hair as he began rocking his
hips to her rhythm, and she lowered her hand to his sac. His
puckered flesh practically writhed beneath her touch as she
gently squeezed and fondled it. She drew him harder into
her mouth, sucking him tight against her tongue. He kept
raising and lowering the knee she wasn't draped across, as if
he couldn't lie still with her working him.

"Honey, I'm gonna come." He released her hair and
grasped the sheet. She wondered if he thought she might pull
back. Silly boy. What insane woman hadn't wanted to savor
every last morsel of him?

His hips jerked and his body pulled taut when the first

taste of him flooded her mouth, and she didn't let up, sucking every precious drop and groaning when her pussy clenched as if lamenting that her mouth was having all the fun. He grasped her hair again, his groans a mingling of endearments and pleasure curses.

Finally he collapsed, spent. She eased her mouth from him and crawled up his body to lie against him. His arms came around her, tenderly pulling her close as his breathing stabilized.

"My God, I think you've performed an exorcism," she whispered after a few silent moments. He kissed her forehead, and she smiled, dragging a hand over her face because it was *numb*. And she needed to make sure it was still there, and that he hadn't caused her to have a stroke.

"I'm in serious danger of keeping you here and not showing you one more inch of Hawaii outside of this bedroom," he said. "But I guess I can't do that in good conscience."

It sounded fine to her, actually.

"Plus," he went on, his voice rumbling in his chest against her ear, "I need my protein or else I'm not gonna be able to keep up with you for the rest of the week. Are you hungry?"

"Famished." Her stomach growled even as she said it.

"That's good to hear," he murmured, smiling beneath the kiss he gave her. "I'll call room service in a second. When I can drag my wasted ass out of bed."

Apparently her brain was slower from lack of nourishment, or all the face-numbing sex, because it took a moment to register what he'd said just a minute ago. *For the rest of the week.*

If she had considered this a one-time thing, she'd been seriously fooling herself. This was exactly what she'd been afraid of. She hadn't wanted to let herself fall. And if Evan Ross fucked her literally senseless for the next four days like he had last night, she didn't see any way out of it.

Getting him out of my system, she thought. *We'll aim for Option Four now. I finally got my chance and that's all I'm doing. We'll go back home and everything will be...*

Be what? Certainly not normal. That was for sure. Her options were dropping like flies.

Oh, God, her job. Evan's trial next week was against her boss, and Jack would need her at court. How in the blue hell was she going to get through that? After a moment, she put that question to Evan, and damn him, he laughed low down and dirty.

"I'll tell you how," he murmured against her ear, sending gooseflesh marching down her arms in waves. "You're not going to wear panties under your skirt. You're going to watch me shred your boss on the floor knowing as soon as we recess for lunch, I'm going to sneak you into my office, bend you over my desk, push up your skirt and fuck your sweet pussy until you can't stand up. I won't let you come until I'm ready for you to."

She struggled to keep him from rendering her mindless. "I'll make you work for it, Mr. Ross."

"Oh, I will. And then you'll go back and do your job trying to defeat me, all flushed and glowing like you are now. I'll love watching you, remembering all the dirty things I just got your pretty mouth to say to me. Knowing that you're still wet from me and that you're still feeling me move inside you. And they'll have no idea about us unless you want them to."

Jesus. It was too late—she loved this man. Waking up beside him in the morning, drinking coffee with him, making love to him. The past few days had done nothing but fill in the gaps of her fantasies. The real Evan had a mile and then some on her make-believe Evan. Oh, God, she was in trouble.

Chapter Seven

Evan hadn't been joking. He could've stayed in bed with her all day. But she'd told him a week or so ago that she wanted to go on a dolphin tour, and their reservation was for this morning. So dolphins she would have.

He had breakfast sent up while she was in the shower, feeling like a cad that he hadn't fed her last night. Food had been the absolute last thing on his mind. She'd turned him into an animal.

When he heard the bathroom door open, he was busy picking up their still-damp clothes from the bedroom floor. "Hey, breakfast is in the liv—"

His voice gave out because he'd looked up as she emerged. It was still a shock to see her utterly naked. She walked over to the closet to survey her clothes, her long black hair spilling down her tanned back. Breath, heart, life itself…seemed to just stop. No, he didn't know if he could ever get used to seeing her like this. But he damn sure liked it.

She seemed to sense his distress and cast a white smile over her delicately curved shoulder. "Okay?"

"Better than." He swallowed.

Her giggle was girlish and she turned back to her task. "Hmm, what to wear?"

"Something I can rip off you with ease."

She ignored that comment, the tease. "We'll snorkel with the dolphins, right? I guess I'll wear my bikini with a sarong."

To hell with the dolphins. And the bikini. And the sarong. He wanted to drag her into bed and spend all day between those smooth tanned thighs. He loved how they tightened on his hips when she was about to come.

She made her selection from the closet and turned toward the bed, her belly ring glittering in the sunlight from the window. "You'd better get ready yourself," she chided, shaking a finger at him.

The sound that left his throat could only be called a growl. Her full lips curled as she stepped into her bikini bottoms and pulled them up, all too quickly hiding that sweetness he only wanted to taste again. But she was so sexy like that, with the little pink scrap of fabric around her hips and her breasts bare and lovely.

"Come here," he murmured.

"Evan!"

"Come here."

She obeyed as he sat on the mattress, and he pulled her between his knees. The scent of honeysuckle filled his nostrils; he knew now that it was her body lotion, which induced rubdown fantasies that could keep him awake at night. He saw her swallow, saw her chest still as her breath caught. Good. Her nipples were almost on the same level as his eyes. He leaned forward and licked one, feeling it pucker against his tongue before moving to the other and eliciting the same response. She moaned, her hands sinking into his hair, her knees going weak—he knew because she had to rest them against the bed to remain standing. He trailed kisses down over her stomach, shifting his position so he could venture lower, nudging beneath the edge of her bottoms. His thumbs gently tugged them down and he traced her clit with his tongue while she sagged over him and sobbed.

Then he stopped, and pulled her bottoms back up. "There. I just had to say good-bye before you covered it all up for the day."

She gasped and burst into laughter. "You—!"

He gave her a teasing smile much like the ones she'd been throwing at him all morning, and tugged her down for a kiss. "Consider it a promise for later," he whispered against her lips.

Evan must have nearly filled up the memory card on his camera with all the pictures he took, but Kelsey snuggling with the dolphins was just the cutest damn sight. She squealed with delight when the first one approached her and let her touch him, and she ran her hand tentatively over his long snout before leaning over to kiss the tip. He chattered happily and bobbed his head and actually looked like he was smiling.

Evan could understand. He didn't think he'd wiped the goofy grin off his face all day.

"He feels like a hardboiled egg," she observed, laughing. "Evan! You've taken enough pics. Come in the water."

"It's just so much fun watching you," he told her.

"Come on, there aren't any sharks," she teased, sending him a wink.

"Ooh, you're gonna get it for airing out my phobias."

"I'm counting on it."

Grinning, he grabbed his mask and snorkel and hopped off the boat into what felt like bathwater. But Kelsey was drawing a crowd around her with her new friend, so she moved aside when several kids crowded around to touch the dolphin. One little boy was reluctant, but Kelsey helped his mom coax him into putting his chubby hand on the dolphin's nose.

Smart, pretty, caring, good with kids. He'd always known that. Dynamite in bed. He hadn't expected that part. In all his imaginings of what sex with her might be like, he'd figured it would be good, safe, warm, sweet. Like her. But it had been nuclear, scalding, incinerating him and every illusion he'd ever held about her.

She was swimming over now to meet him, and only then did he realize he'd stopped making his way toward her. He was only staring at her.

"You okay?" she asked once she'd reached him.

"Yeah."

"That was really cool."

He cleared his throat, trying to get a grasp on the emotions twisting their way through his chest before he said something sappy. "I should bring you in the winter so we can whale watch. You'd love it. We saw a humpback last time I was here."

With her hair slicked straight back, her strong cheekbones and delicate forehead were beautifully accentuated. Stunning. The vibrant blue of the water brought out deep shades of twilight in her gray eyes. She was radiant this morning, glowing. Apparently he had a good effect on her. "So you think you'd want to do that, huh?" she asked, giving his arm a little pinch.

"Absolutely," he said, and meant it.

"Well, I'd like that."

It was by no means any kind of commitment, but it perhaps hinted at one. He took a breath. The world around him was postcard perfect. He'd seen it all before, but he had never appreciated it nearly as much as he did now, with her. The realization was exhilarating and it scared the hell out of him. She'd always meant so much to him that taking this leap seemed an insane risk. He wanted to tell himself they had time, not to rush it, but he didn't think he could stop himself. With her, at the point they'd arrived at last night, it was all or nothing. They couldn't go back to the way they were before.

He only hoped he knew what the hell he was getting himself into.

After snorkeling and admiring the coral reefs and the sea turtles that came over to investigate their presence, they loaded back on the boat with the other tourists. Kelsey snuggled into Evan's side and he wrapped his arm around her shoulders. She loved the weight of it there. She loved the beauty all around her. The sun warming her skin, the wind tossing her curls dry. Life was definitely worth living at times like this. If she had one care back in the real world, she couldn't think of it right now.

They were just resting that way, admiring the emerald greens, sapphire blues and sprinklings of pink slipping past them, when her cell phone rang in the bag by her sandaled feet. She leaned over to retrieve it and chuckled when she read the display. "It's Lisa. She better not have given birth without me."

"You know, I terrorized that girl when she was Jack's paralegal."

"I've heard. Over and over again." Kelsey laughed as she flipped her phone open. "Lisa! Don't tell me."

Lisa sounded tired, but content. "Sorry, girl. It's not my fault. She wouldn't wait for you."

She grabbed Evan's hand in excitement. "Oh my God, congratulations! When?"

"Last night. C-section this time. Can you believe it? By the third, you'd think they could fall out like paratroopers.

But noooo. I told Daniel my uterus is officially retired. I don't think he was too heartbroken about it."

Kelsey had been laughing since the "paratrooper" remark. "But everything went okay?"

"Aside from being gutted like a fish? Sure. And she's adorable, of course. We named her Meagan Rose like we'd planned. Seven-and-a-half pounds, lots of dark hair, big blue eyes. Lungs like mine."

"God help you."

"Tell me about it. So my trauma is done. How are things with you?"

"Great, it's gorgeous here. Beautiful weather. We're having a blast."

Lisa's voice took on a conspirator's tone. "And how are the waves?"

Kelsey was amazed Lisa gave a damn about "waves" and all that entailed at a time like this. And she supposed it would look weird to Evan if she started rattling off words like *tsunami*. Or *storm surge*. Rogue wave of *Poseidon* proportions, flipping her ship upside down. She kept her voice as level as possible. "They're *awesome*."

Lisa trilled with laughter for a split second before giving a grunt of pain. Poor thing. "You dirty hag. I told you. You'll learn to listen to me one of these days, I know about this stuff. Is Evan right there? Put his cute butt on the phone. I feel the need to torture him a bit, especially after he called me Pregzilla last time I saw him."

Crap. "Lisa, don't…"

"Oh, I won't let on that I know you're having the wild monkey sex."

"Hang on." Kelsey held her phone over to Evan. "She wants to talk to you."

"*Really*." He grinned and grabbed it. "Lisa Scott! Dammit, woman, what are you doing having my baby while I'm out of town? I'm outraged."

Even from several inches away and over her own laughter Kelsey heard Lisa squeal. Evan wore his most devilish grin as he listened to Lisa's most likely obscenity-laden retort. As sharp as she was, she never could quite top him. Kelsey had a sinking feeling that *now* Lisa wouldn't be able to resist nailing Evan with what she knew. The conversation was getting several amused glances from the others on the boat. She could only hear Evan's half of it.

"Playing with dolphins… Yes, I'll get you a picture of that… You know I'm taking really good care of her, not letting her dance on any tabletops. You know how she is." He laughed as Kelsey smacked his arm, and after a few more minutes he handed the phone back over after sincerely congratulating Lisa on her new baby.

"Sometimes I cannot believe that crazy man is the same one who can make the entire jury box weep while Jack snaps pencils in his bare hands. I thought I pulled out a staple or two laughing at him just now."

"I know." Kelsey had to bite her tongue to keep from adding *Isn't he amazing?*

"Are you sure you can handle him?"

"Well, I'm doing my best."

"Good girl. You know, despite my new wriggling bundle of joy, I was tired and sore and feeling just a little depressed earlier, but you guys have perked me right up. I wish you the best of luck, Kelsey, I really do. I always thought you two would be awesome, if you could just get it together."

"Thank you. I can't wait to meet my new niece."

They hung up and Kelsey put her phone back in her bag, a smile lingering on her lips. "I'm so glad for them."

"They're good people." Evan pulled her back to his side and pressed a kiss to her ear. She shifted a bit and wrapped her arms around him.

"I don't know what I would've done without them after everything that happened. I need to buy something for the baby while we're here."

"We'll go look around the shops this afternoon, if you want." He pointed out to the water, where one of the dolphins was putting on a show for them, as if imploring them not to leave. Kelsey grabbed her camera and snapped a picture of it.

"That'll be fun." Looking for baby clothes with Evan. Things just kept getting weirder.

"I hope I didn't upset you, joking around with her like that," he murmured in her ear. "I didn't really think before I said it. But that kind of stuff always gets her riled up."

"You didn't. I thought it was funny." Kelsey bit her lip on a retort that probably would have distressed him. She wasn't some kind of delicate mental case who couldn't take a joke, even if that seemed to be the situation. The teasing was just his way, no different than how he'd acted since she'd known him. But his concern touched her, so she let it slide. It was the first time he'd ever shown any in that particular area. Normally Evan didn't seem to give a damn what people thought about him.

The constant stream of innuendo he could keep up with anyone was one reason Kelsey had never thought he was serious any time he flirted with her. Why she'd always known how dangerous it was for her to feel the way she did about him. It might have bothered her more if she didn't know how loyal he always was to the one he was with. Her heart gave funny little flip-flops at the thought of being that person for him now.

The chatter on the boat went on around them, but in his arms she was in her own world. The hum of the engine and the spray of the water were real, but the only thing that mattered to her was the solidity of his chest beneath her cheek. She could've slept here, feeling safe as a kitten. She might have dozed for a bit; fuzzy, senseless thoughts were drifting lazily through her mind.

When she finally lifted her head, they were pulling in to dock. A couple of girls were sitting across from them, very pretty, perhaps college age. They had been laughing the most at Evan's conversation with Lisa. One was smiling at them now.

"You guys are so cute together. Are you on your honeymoon?" she asked.

Kelsey felt her cheeks redden and started to shake her head.

"We're just friends," Evan said teasingly, giving her a light pinch on her side so that she giggled and pushed at him. Then he caught her in a kiss that could have straightened her hair.

Somehow Kelsey heard the remark the girl made to her companion. "I think I need a friend like that."

They shopped until she was ready to drop. By the time the sun began to set, little Meagan had the makings of a wardrobe… that would last her first six months of life, anyway. It seemed once they started, they couldn't stop.

Evan had been adorable in his excitement, almost as if he were buying for his own kid. Kelsey had a warmth in her chest she sometimes found it difficult to breathe through without letting it spill out in a declaration of love that might ruin the tranquility of their day. It seemed so fragile, this safety she'd found with him. So precious she feared it slipping right through her fingers and shattering forever. She supposed it would feel that way until there was some certainty between them, yet asking for it was the very thing she knew could push it further from her grasp.

"Well, I think you bought entirely too much frilly pink,"

he teased in the car on the way back to the resort.

"Hey, Lisa did have a *girl*."

"So? My daughter will wear camouflage. She'll be tough. I'll take her hunting. She'll whip all the boys."

"Yeah, right," Kelsey laughed. "I didn't see too much camouflage back there. I bet one thing is for sure about any daughter of yours: she'll have her daddy wrapped right here." She held up one pinky finger.

"Can't argue with that." He flipped the blinker to turn into their hotel parking lot. "Did you and Todd ever talk about having kids?"

"Not really. It was one of those topics that, when it got brought up, the subject was changed pretty quick."

"I don't suppose I have to guess who changed it."

She shrugged. "You can't fault someone for not wanting to have kids. It's a personal choice."

"Courtney didn't want kids, either. I didn't find this out until I'd already asked her to marry me. We went around and around about it. Not that I wanted them right away, but you know. Someday. I hated to break off an engagement over something I hoped she'd change her mind about eventually."

"Sounds like they're a match made in heaven, then. Or some other, hotter place," Kelsey grumbled, facing out her window. "Can I ask you something? You don't have to answer."

"Shoot."

"I've seen you get pretty serious about a few girls. What was so different about Courtney that made her the one you asked to marry you?"

He seemed to debate for a moment, so at least he wasn't going to shut her down. She just wondered if he was going to evade the question. "I don't know if it was so much that she was different, or if I was."

"What do you mean?"

"You know. Established, getting older, tired of playing the field. Ready to settle down, I guess. She just happened to be the one that was there."

"It had to be more than that."

"Well, yeah. We had a good time together, got along for the most part, families liked one another…" He trailed away as he pulled into an empty parking space. Once stopped, he turned to look at her. "You're really wanting to ask if I was in love with her, aren't you?"

She shrugged, her cheeks starting to burn. "It's not my business. But yeah."

"I can't say that I was. I had feelings for her, of course, but I see what a huge mistake I'd have been making to marry her. I think I knew already, in the back of my mind, before it all went to hell. I'd have been doomed to contentment. Nothing more."

Evan was one of the lucky ones, to dodge that bullet. If only she could have been so fortunate.

"Hey." He reached over to stroke her hair. "Didn't mean to dredge anything up there."

She turned to look at him, at his beautiful, precious face. The glow of the sunset sparked in his eyes. She had to take a breath. "No, it's fine. I'm the one who asked. You're right. I need to move past it all."

He toyed with her fingers, slowly rubbing each in turn with his thumb. "You really haven't, have you?"

She shrugged, her gaze on their joined hands. "It was such an upheaval. My mom begged me to move back home, and I couldn't. I told her I thought one more huge change in my life would break me down completely." He continued his caresses, letting her go on. "And all the cruel words that got thrown around. It was a rollercoaster, civil one minute, hateful the next. I have only one thing good to say about it: thank *God* we didn't have kids."

"It probably was for the best," he said soothingly. Damn him, he was using his prosecutor voice. The one he used with distraught victims on the stand. He must think she was a regular head case.

"I know I'm not the only woman in the world who's gone through a divorce. I'm not the only woman who's ever been cheated on. I wish I could shake it off like other people seem to."

"From the eye that doesn't know any better, you have. Whenever I see you around, you're always smiling, dealing just fine. So maybe everyone else isn't as together as you think they are, either."

She sniffed, proud of herself that she wasn't crying. She didn't want to start now. "You are."

"You think so, huh? I have my pain, too."

"You hide it well, then."

"My point exactly."

"I must be terrible at hiding mine. At least I have been this week." She looked at him, feeling as if there were a crack in the door to his soul and she wanted to open it wide. "Tell me what hurts you?"

He blew out a breath. "I can't, honey. Maybe someday."

"Why not? I'm an open freakin' book here, and—"

"A lot of things hurt me. What they did…yeah, it hurt like hell. I got Courtney home that night and I couldn't get near her. Not that I was afraid I'd hurt her or anything crazy like that, but I couldn't stand to have her anywhere close to me. She was following me around begging me to listen to her and I couldn't even deal with the sound of her voice."

She nodded. She understood completely. Except Todd had never begged. Evan wasn't telling her everything, but she wouldn't press the issue. It hurt her to know there was something he didn't trust her with, but she'd done the very same thing to him last night.

"There is one thing I need to tell you, Kelsey. It might matter to you and it might not, but it's not right for me to keep it from you."

Her pulse rate doubled. "What?"

"They aren't together anymore."

Good. Serves them right. "Oh. Why not?"

"She says it's because he misses you."

Kelsey scoffed. "That's unlikely."

"Do you really think so? Because, honey…" His stroking fingers moved up her bare arm, to her shoulder. "I'd miss you. I'd miss you like crazy. I don't see how any man with a beating heart and rushing blood wouldn't." The fingers of his other hand skimmed her thigh, brushing up just under the hem of her skirt. That barest touch had her wanting to open her legs for him here in the car. His mouth moved swift to cover hers, a sensation she'd been longing for all day. She put her hand on the side of his neck, stroking his flesh, feeling the muscles work as his lips moved over hers with feverish insistence.

"Bed?" she murmured against them, and felt rather than saw his smile.

"No. I think first I'm taking you out to dinner." And he chuckled at her frustrated growl.

Chapter Eight

Their table was nestled in the corner of the outdoor section, where the wind could caress her bare shoulders and wreak its havoc on her hair. Kelsey didn't mind. She found she actually liked it. Since last night, Evan couldn't seem to keep his hands out of her curls. Having it wild and tumbling around her face made her feel sexy. Brash and brazen.

It wasn't just her hair. It was the way his gaze lingered on her flesh. It was his nearness, the memory of him inside her, taking her to heights never before accessed. She still felt lush and sensitive and wanton. He sat to her left, and she wanted to get her hands on him under this tablecloth. She found herself inching her left knee toward him, trying to find contact with solid muscle. But it was a frustrating effort, so she tried to focus on the scenery.

"This is beautiful," she said, gazing out at the waves rolling in on the beach, the whitecaps glowing in the moonlight. "I never could have taken a trip like this without you."

Evan sipped his wine. "Sure you could have."

She cocked an eyebrow at him. "Oh yeah? How do you

figure?"

"You can do anything you want to. I know times are tight for you right now. But it won't always be that way."

"You really are a glass-is-half-full kinda guy, aren't you? I always knew it, but really, sometimes it's just too much."

"Why?"

"Oh, I wouldn't change that about you," she said quickly. "I love it. But I don't think you know what it's like to have to struggle."

"Well, if you're speaking strictly about finances, I guess you're right. But if you're thinking it isn't sometimes a struggle for me to keep my rose-colored glasses after the things I've seen on the job, my dear, you're mistaken." He chucked her gently under her chin. "Some days it takes everything I am to walk into that courtroom."

The breeze blew a strand of his hair across his forehead and she reached up to move it away. It was becoming one of her favorite things to do. "Sorry. I need more optimism in my life, I know it. And I know you've seen some terrible things. I would never want your job to turn you into a cynic."

His eyes were distant for a moment, and she knew she'd just conjured up images of gruesome murders and sexual assaults and child abuse. *Great job, Kels.* "It won't," he said. "If it ever starts to, I can always do something else. See? There's always a way out."

A little candle flickered in its votive cup in the center of their table. She found herself mesmerized by the little pinprick of light reflected in Evan's eyes as he looked at her. He must have seen something similar in hers, because he was studying her intently. Then his fingers crept over her bare shoulder, pushing away a curl. She shivered at the touch.

"Do you remember a lot about college?" he asked. "About stuff we used to do?"

The unexpected question made her laugh. "Of course.

I think I remember every minute." Every minute with him, anyway. "It all went by too fast."

"You must have missed a week of classes to take care of me that week I had the flu. I think about that a lot. I came out of my NyQuil coma to find most of the notes from my classes there waiting for me and an extension on my Constitutional Law paper."

"I felt so bad for you. You were miserable."

"Yeah—well, it's hard to remember a lot, with the angel of death hovering over my bed at the time." He grinned. "But I had an angel of mercy fighting him off. Shoving chicken soup and orange juice down my throat. Keeping me bundled up and taking my temperature every ten minutes. I swear, Kelsey, I don't know what I'd have done without you. Imagine how terrible I felt when you caught it the very next week."

She shrugged, then laughed. "You returned the favor. If you'd left me to rot in my room, then I might've been pissed."

And she couldn't in a millennium be upset over just *how* she suspected she'd contracted his death flu. It had been enough to give her shivers for years…and even now. Early on in his illness, she'd been particularly worried about him one night when his fever spiked. She hadn't wanted to leave him. Whichever girl he'd been seeing at the time had been terrified of catching what he had and refused to come around. Evan had fallen into a fitful sleep watching Letterman, and Kelsey had lain in his bed next to him, watching him toss and turn and groan, until she dozed off.

In the middle of the night, she'd awakened with his feverish arm across her waist, pulling her to him, his breath hot against her ear. He'd been sound asleep, but still reaching for her. She'd let him snuggle against her and absorb her warmth, because even though he was burning her through their clothes he'd been shivering like he was freezing. So had she, just from his nearness. She'd wanted so desperately to turn and kiss him, put her hands all over him, germs and all. He probably wouldn't have even known who she was at that moment. The half-terrified virgin in her had held her still.

When she'd awakened later, she'd found him on the couch, and the pain of that had been brutal. Still, those few minutes in his arms had been worth the misery of the illness that followed. Over the years, her mind had taken that moment and expanded it into some pretty delicious fantasies.

"After I caught it, you practically wrote a paper for me, didn't you?" she asked, forcing herself to snap out of it. She had reality now, and it was ten times more delicious. "I'm like you, I barely remember anything about that week." Except for him only leaving her side to attend the most crucial classes, and only then because she begged him to go since he'd already missed so much.

"Your prof wouldn't budge on the due date because you'd had over a month to do it already, but some of that you'd spent taking care of me. So I outlined your Juvenile Justice paper for you. You did the rest. Though I did proofread it, and honestly, it looked like a monkey had written it. In the dark. So I fixed it for you."

"Jeopardizing our future careers," she said, shaking her head.

He waved a hand dismissively. "They never would have figured it out. I looked back through some of your old papers to see if you had any quirks I needed to know about. I can be pretty crafty when I need to be."

"So I've seen," she said, leaning forward for a kiss. He moved to meet her, only he paused inches away.

"You've always been there for me. It's never gone unappreciated, Kelsey, even if I neglect to tell you often enough."

"I know," she whispered. "You didn't have to say anything. You were always there for me, too."

"I always wondered why you gave a damn about me."

She sat back. "Why would you wonder that?"

"Because I was a shit back then, and you know it." He laughed. "When it came to most of my relationships and even my friendships, I was the proverbial bull in a china shop."

"I never saw that in you. I'll admit, that day in class when Dr. Roberts assigned us to work together, and I didn't know you, I thought, 'Great, I know who'll be doing all the work on this project. Me.' Because every day you walked in class like you owned it and you sat with a horde of giggling females around you, always flirting with them."

He was shaking his head self-deprecatingly now, covering his eyes. If the lighting weren't so dim out here, she would swear he was blushing. She couldn't tell him that aside from the dread she'd felt toward doing one hundred percent of the work that lay ahead, her heart had flipped over on itself at the thought of even *possibly* spending time with him. He was the most beautiful man she'd ever seen. "But then I got to know you," she went on. "You weren't stuck on yourself at all. I thought you were amazing, and I felt bad for stereotyping you like I did at first. I was so glad that you still seemed to want to be friends with me after we were finished working together."

"You really kept my feet on the ground back then. You came into my life at a time when I could've thrown it all away."

"What do you mean?"

"I mean I was slipping. I was twenty. There was always a party to go to or people to see. It was becoming more important than what I was there for. Then you came along. Cracking your whip, keeping me in line."

She smoothed her napkin in her lap, a little smile curling her lips. "Are you saying I helped you become the man you are today?"

Evan threw back his head and laughed. "I guess so, honey. God only knows where I'd be without you." He took another sip of wine, his gaze meeting hers over the rim.

She wanted to ask him, if she was so important, why he hadn't wanted her back then. Why, no matter what she did, he seemed to look at her as nothing more than a little sister. It wasn't that she was an ugly-duckling-turned-swan case. She was barely any different now than she'd been at twenty. Maybe a few more wrinkles, and just after her divorce she'd discovered her first gray hair, which had sent her into another tailspin. But the same twenty-year-old Evan had ignored sexually, he'd ravished at thirty. It shouldn't matter anymore, except that she still had a few old wounds from it that had been left to fester all these years. They'd been reopened after the debacle her life had become.

Kelsey couldn't ask him about any of that. She might not like what he had to say.

Their food arrived, and she tried to focus on just how heavenly her coconut shrimp tasted. *Exist in the moment*, she told herself. Awesome food, awesome scenery and the company she most craved on this earth. Forget old hurts, don't anticipate new ones. It was hard for her, who'd grown so accustomed to looking at the dark side of things. To waiting for the axe to fall. She wished she could be like Evan, who did see that glass as half full and would argue his case to death. Just for that alone, she admired him more than she could ever tell him.

He fascinated her. Every move he made, her eyes followed it. For the thousandth time, she wondered what it was about him that kept her so riveted. Why she shivered at the simple way he held his wineglass, or his fork, or his pen when he signed the credit card slip with a flourish. Why those little things never struck her from other people. Never had she salivated just watching the way Todd's lips touched the rim of his glass.

Kelsey was taking a sip of her own water when Evan's

hand slid over her naked knee, and she nearly spit it out at the shock of his touch. Maybe *that* was why. She was imagining that touch on her flesh, not some inanimate object that couldn't appreciate it. His fingertips slid beneath the hem of her flimsy black-and-white print skirt and over the flesh of her inner thigh, leaving little trails of fire. She set her glass down, trying to retain her composure when she wanted to erupt out of her chair and straddle him where he sat.

"You have the softest skin I've ever touched," he murmured, and it was only then she dared to look him in the eyes. In the dimness, they were dark, unreadable. As if there was hardly a sliver of green around his pupils. Aroused.

"Evan…" She trailed away when his fingers crept as far up her leg as they could without him leaning over and looking too obvious. It wasn't far enough. She inched down in her seat, just barely, surely imperceptibly, and spread her legs, thanking God this tablecloth was so long. His touch slid higher. Still not enough. "Oh, God."

"I think we've tortured ourselves enough today," he said, watching her. "Are you ready to head back?"

Her breath was a shudder. Last night, every minute of it, was a blazing beacon in her thoughts. She wanted that again. All of it. Unable to speak, she nodded.

He remembered everything about that night he'd been so sick. He remembered waking up with her in his arms, so hard it hurt. When it became impossible to lie still next to her without the urge to grind his aching cock into her backside, he'd had to get up, gulp more Tylenol and crash on the couch. She'd looked so tired he hadn't wanted to wake her.

All that day one single scary thought had been at the forefront of his mind: *This girl is wife material.* It had been thoughts like that one that sent him running for the hills, desperate to replace it with rationalizations. *This is your very good, very sweet, very* virginal *friend. Yes, she's pretty. Yes, she's perfect. She's everything you should want to find in someone. Which is why you're going to keep your dick far, far away from her. You have a girlfriend. Don't do it, don't be that guy.*

The years had only removed all those inhibitions. "Wife material" wasn't such a terrifying concept anymore. Someone who was perfect for him was to be treasured, not run from. No girlfriends anywhere in sight. And he couldn't wait to get inside Kelsey again.

Evan had always found it quite hard, though not at all unpleasant, to drive with a scorching hot woman trying to crawl into his lap. Planting nibbling, sucking little kisses along his throat. Her hands doing unspeakable things in unspeakable places, driving him out of his mind. God, but Kelsey was going to get it when he could stop this vehicle. He only hoped he could wait to get into the suite to give it to her. She didn't know how close she was to inducing him to pull over into some dark lot, drag her onto his lap and impale her on his cock right here where he sat. He didn't think she would complain. And God knew at this point he probably wouldn't last long enough to get them busted. She had him ready to blow.

"Honey," he groaned as she nibbled his earlobe and gave his stiff shaft a long, hard stroke through his pants. "I'm concerned for the safety of the public right now."

"I trust you," she murmured, moving her lips around to the corner of his mouth. "I think the public is in good hands."

"Mmm, and I think you're about to be."

"God, Evan, I'm so wet."

He nearly drove off the road. The need to take his hand off the wheel and investigate her claim was almost more than he could resist. It would be easy; she was so close, half kneeling in her seat, and if they hadn't almost reached the hotel he'd probably exhort her to sit and put her seatbelt on. In the interest of safety, and all. But what she was doing felt so good, and they'd be there in a minute...

He managed to squeeze into a darkened space without grazing any other vehicle. It was a miracle. Kelsey's hands were under his shirt, her lips wet and hot on the side of his neck. He was hard enough to break rocks, barely managing to shove the gearshift into Park before he grabbed her face between his palms and kissed her deeply, thoroughly. She moaned and crawled over him, her hands twisting in his hair.

So easy, it would be so easy to unzip his pants, tug her panties to the side and slide up inside her. He pushed his hand up her skirt to cup her ass and realized it would be easier than he thought. She wasn't wearing any panties.

Christ. He had to get a grip, or this would be over before it started.

"Sweetie, let's go inside," he whispered. "We have all night. I'm not going anywhere."

Her eyes were wild in the dim green glow from the dashboard lights, her lips dark and full from the pressure of his. "I want you so much. I want to give you everything."

The words drew out something primeval and possessive inside him, the need to cherish her and protect her and above all else, claim her as his own. Erase all memory that she'd ever belonged to anyone else, that she'd ever given *anything* to a man who didn't appreciate her and didn't treasure her with his entire being. She was the one who deserved everything, everything he had to give.

The journey up to their room was the longest of her life, and the click of the door behind them shutting out the rest of the world, the sweetest sound she'd ever heard aside from his voice.

She dropped her purse to the floor and toed off her sandals so the thick carpet could well between her toes. Even the swish of her skirt around her legs was sensuous as she turned into his embrace, standing on her tiptoes to reach his lips with hers. His arms encircled her waist, lifting her against him to ease their distance in height. It was her natural response to wrap her legs around his waist, to better press the throbbing apex between her thighs tight against his erection. She moved her hips, loving the friction, stoking it, their mutual groans mingling as their mouths did.

This had to be wrong. Nothing that wasn't damningly sinful could feel so good. The man was the devil, to do this to her, to turn her into this madwoman strung out on his touch. As he gathered her weight higher in his arms and planted her back hard against the wall of their living room, she was limp as a dishrag, clinging to him to hold her up. Still, she operated on enough strength and instinct to reach down and unbutton his pants, fingers desperate to enclose his cock, to stroke it so that he made more of those delectable sounds. And then to guide it deep, deep inside her.

His flesh was hot and hard in her hand. He closed his eyes, his head falling back as she used both hands, one then the other, to glide over him from base to tip. He was already damp with his pre-come, and it thrilled her that she did this to him. At the feel of his girth in her hands, her own moisture had doubled so that the inside of her thighs felt dewy. The empty ache in her womb intensified, and she tried to adjust herself to take him. He lifted her higher, shifted his hips and teased her clit with the head of his cock, sawing it back and forth so that her bud tightened and pulsed.

"Oh, God!" she cried. She fisted his shirt in her hands until she almost ripped it.

"Not yet," he murmured, halting his motions amid her cries of protest. Those cries stopped abruptly when he plunged into her, because for a moment, she completely ceased to be. Every cell in her body imploded with agonized pleasure. Every ensuing thrust drove a cry from her throat, and she tried to meet them, to give back to him, but her movements were pathetic echoes of his. Everywhere she was weak and helpless, he was strong and rigid and straining.

Wrong, wrong, this has to be wrong...

"Don't leave me," he murmured, looking into her unfocused, barely seeing eyes. She recognized her own words from last night.

"I'm right here," she said, more of a whimper than a declaration.

"Do you know how good you feel?"

"I hope...as good as...you feel... Oh, Evan..."

His lips encircled her nipple through her black halter top, the moisture soaking through to her flesh. She'd foregone a bra tonight, as well.

"Should've taken this fucking thing off," he growled, and even through the pleasure wreaking havoc on her thoughts, she laughed. Then his teeth grazed her nipple through her shirt and she lost all capacity to make any sound beyond cavewoman grunts.

Evan slowed his movements and adjusted her weight so that he could pull her away from the wall. She clung to him as he walked their entangled bodies over to the couch, then toppled them over on it.

"Put your foot on the floor," he whispered, and she did, opening herself up wide to him. He grasped her other calf and lifted it against the back of the couch, holding it in place with his arm braced on the back. "Pull up your shirt." She did, slowly, running her hands over both breasts as she went. Her cheeks burned hot as fire, her breath came in wild pants. If she didn't get a grasp on it, she feared passing out.

"Jesus," he murmured. "Keep doing that." As she caressed herself, shuddering beneath him, he watched her hands move before lowering his lips to one pink, distended nipple peeking between her fingers. His tongue flickered over it, grazing her knuckles along with her pebbled flesh, soft and wet. She moved her fingers underneath the swell to give him easier access, and he responded by sucking it until she thought it would burst. But he held his hips torturously still, surely staving off his own orgasm. Thinking of her first. That knowledge sweetened her, but she was still desperate for him to move again, to fuck her like this. She waited on him, sobbing her impatience. He was still thick and pulsing inside her. Oh, if he didn't move soon she would have to…

"I'm finding it difficult," he said suddenly, "to deal with the knowledge that you get even tighter just before you come."

The words jarred loose her desperation for him. "Please, Evan."

He drew a deep breath and kissed her, his mouth playing gently across first her top lip and then her bottom, tender caresses she tried to capture, to pull in, because she wanted his tongue in her mouth. He evaded her, even when she tried to raise her head, a wicked little grin curving the corners of his lips. Almost imperceptibly, he began withdrawing his shaft from her, slow as the moon crawled across the sky outside. She tossed her head on the arm of the couch. She needed it back, and faster, she needed it faster…

"I love seeing you this way too much," he confessed. "I never thought I'd be here. I don't want it to end, honey."

Kelsey didn't either, truth be known. She wanted to be here with him, like this, from now on. Never having to face the world. These moments were precious, too precious to rush, even for the promise of earth-shattering pleasure hovering just beyond her reach. It would be over too soon.

Would it *all* be over?

The thought of going home in a few days was sobering, but Evan began to move inside her, and her thoughts splintered and shattered. His lips swirled around hers once and then claimed them fully, his tongue sinking past her teeth. He tasted warm and spicy and as intoxicating as the wine he'd drunk. She went liquid, clutching him, the pleasure centers in her brain delighting in every place the two of them touched, joined. He was like a drug in her system.

His thrusts grew stronger in increments. Her legs ached from being spread so wide, but it was a small price to pay for the thick, gliding shaft working her to ecstasy between them. The heat reached a fever pitch, and she turned her face away, not wanting him to see the emotions that crossed her face. She was going to lose her mind, absolutely lose it...

"Sweetheart, don't," he whispered. She'd forgotten. He'd called her out on that last night, too. It was so hard to let go while he watched. Even though he seemed to take most of her control away from her, she still tried to grasp a little piece of it with her bare fingernails, to safeguard her heart. When he wrenched it away, stripped her bare like this, she was defenseless.

"Evan..."

"Don't hide from me. You know me. I won't hurt you."

Oh, but he could. He held all the power in the universe to crush her heart into oblivion, and she was giving it to him willingly. She let him in anyway, turning her face up to him for a reassuring kiss as she felt the overwhelming tightening of all her muscles, of her body clenching around him, sucking at the pleasure he poured into her. It all swirled into one blazing hot pinpoint and exploded. Her foot came off the floor and she wrapped her leg around him, enfolding him fully in her arms so that he couldn't have extricated himself had he wanted to. She wanted every drop of him.

Somehow, in the midst of it all, it occurred to her just how unconvincing all her fake orgasms had been with her ex. She hadn't screamed then, she hadn't gone stiff and tight all over nor had she produced these fluttering contractions deep inside her womb—she didn't think any amount of theatrics could fabricate those. They were from him, from what he did to her body. As he came with a burning rush inside her and a groan that wrenched her heart, she held him tight and shuddered through it with him.

Kelsey didn't know how long they lay like that, still and silent with her cradling him beside her as her muscles dissolved into bliss. It wasn't comfortable, but it was close, and it was what she needed. He stroked her face and hair and body until he dozed, and she slipped into unconsciousness only to awaken to him carrying her to bed. They made slow, sleepy love in utter darkness and collapsed for the rest of the night, Evan holding her just as he had all those years ago, curling her body against his warmth, his breath near her ear.

Chapter Nine

The rain poured down in a thick, gray curtain. Evan watched it from his seat on their private lanai, where he was sheltered from the deluge by the floor several feet above his head. He was still getting splashed a bit, but it felt good. He propped his bare feet up on the wet railing and sipped his coffee. Kelsey thought he was insane that he liked to go outside in the rain so much, yet he thought it wouldn't take much persuasion to get her to join him sometime. His favorite place in the world to be—besides here, right now—was on his front porch, watching a storm. He certainly wouldn't mind being warm in bed with Kelsey, but he hadn't talked to his mother all week, so he'd walked out here to call and check in with her.

"I went by your house to check on your brother," his mom was saying.

"Tell me it wasn't a pile of rubble."

"No, no. It looks like Brian's taking care of things. I was impressed."

"No evidence of wild drunken headbanging riots? Did you lay eyes on my dogs? Were they skeletal? Or carved up and sacrificed to some pagan god?"

She laughed. "They were fine. Brian said to tell you he would have a bucket of ice waiting for you when you got back. He said you'd know what it meant, and I hope so, because *I* don't want to know."

Well, well. Brian was going to be sorely disappointed. Evan grinned, tipping his chair back on two legs. "Yeah, he's just being typical Brian."

"Are you outside? Is that rain?" his mom asked.

"Yeah."

"Ah. Sorry you're having bad weather."

He gazed down on the beach, where the waves continued to roll in through the gray haze, and palm fronds jiggled and danced with water drops. "Today is the first time we've had it. It hasn't been so bad. We've just been lazing around waiting for it to clear up."

"Surely you can find something to do? Don't let Kelsey get bored," she chided.

"I'm not, don't you worry about that. She's laid back like me."

"So you are having a good time with her?"

"I, uh…I don't think I quite expected to have such a good time."

There was a pause. "Why do I get the feeling by those few words that other things have happened you didn't expect?"

Evan laughed. "I knew I wouldn't get anything by you. Not that I wanted to try."

"Evan Giovanni Ross!" Her words dissolved in a string of Italian that made him cringe. He wasn't normally the son who caused Gianna to revert to her native language in anger. "I knew this would happen."

"What? You like Kelsey, don't you?"

"You know I *adore* her. I love her. That is what bothers me."

"Why?"

"Because if it doesn't work out with her, then you've really lost something. We all have."

"The thought of that scares me, too. But I can't go back and change what's happened here." He drew a breath. "I know I don't have a great track record, but I'm trying. I tried with the last one, remember?"

"You didn't want to marry Courtney." She sighed heavily. "Sometimes I don't know what it will take to get me grandbabies."

Here we go again, he thought. "Mom, I'm not deliberately trying to stand in your way of that. But hey, you never know, maybe it'll take a woman who's already been in my life for ten years, who I know I have a good time with, and who" — *rocks my whole world in bed* — "already knows me better than anyone else."

"But your best friend's ex?"

"Ex-best friend's ex. I don't have any notions of loyalty toward Todd Jacobs anymore."

"I know, Evan, but you were best man at their wedding. Don't you think that looks bizarre?"

"I really don't give a damn. Come on, Mom. You did crazy things for love, didn't you? You moved to a whole other country for my dad."

"If it's love, then you have my wholehearted blessing."

Man, she'd pounced on that. He turned and looked through the glass doors, worried for a moment that Kelsey might be able to hear him. He didn't want her to think he was having to defend their relationship to his mother. There was no doubt in his mind that once the potential scandal they would incite blew over, his mom would be overjoyed for him and Kelsey to be together.

If it ever had a chance to go there. Kelsey still had hang-ups. He saw them all the time. There was something she was afraid of, and it made her not want to open up to him. Hell, it was probably like his mother had insinuated. Why would Kelsey give her heart to him when, judging by his past foul-ups, there was almost a one hundred percent chance he would take it and run? He couldn't sustain a relationship.

But he'd sustained theirs so far. She'd been the one person he couldn't imagine living without. The months they'd spent hardly speaking, both of them humiliated and heartbroken, had torn him apart. He'd wanted them to heal over their time together, not slash open all new wounds. But at least she hadn't seemed fazed by the news that Todd and Courtney had broken up.

His mom finally wished him well and hung up, so he wandered back into the living room, his damp pajama pants clinging to his calves. Kelsey was in the kitchen cleaning up, wearing one of his shirts and nothing else. It was stark white against her tan skin, long-sleeved, and reached almost to her knees. She'd rolled up the sleeves and only fastened a few of the buttons, so the V at her throat left just the first swells of her breasts exposed.

She looked at him and smiled, wiping off the counter. Maybe she *was* bored. They hadn't been messy. "What is it?"

He'd been staring. "Just admiring my shirt."

"Oh." She laughed, glancing down at herself. "I hope you don't mind."

"How could I? It looks better on you than it ever could on me. In fact, you should only wear my clothes from now on." He approached her and drew her close. Her arms went around his waist, and he gently smoothed her hair back with both hands, gazing down at her upturned face. Her eyes matched the skies outside. Stormy gray.

"You're wet," she said, stroking the bare skin of his back.

"You're beautiful."

Kelsey's soft pink lips curled. "How is your mom? I

haven't seen her in a long time. I guess the last time was… well, when I saw her out having lunch with Courtney."

"When was that?"

"Oh, way back. Before. You know."

"Yeah. She's fine. She sends her love, and asks you to please keep me in line."

"How am I doing so far?"

"I think I'm pretty well lined out, don't you?" He pulled her closer so she could feel exactly what her nearness did to him, and she giggled and swatted at him.

"You're insatiable!"

Only for you. "You're not tired of me already, are you?"

"God, no."

"Good. Because you know, rainy day, nothing to do, stuck here all morning…I can think of *lots* we could do right now." He trailed a finger down between her breasts, and her eyes closed.

"Are you sure this is something we should get into?"

His movements stilled, and he stared at her until her eyes slowly opened. Maybe she'd heard him after all. "I think it's a little late for that question. What's on your mind?"

"I know you said nothing we do together could be wrong, and I want to believe that, but…"

"How *can* it be wrong, honey? We're both free to do whatever we damn well please." He looked her hard in the eyes, trying to delve in there, trying to get to the heart of her protests. But she managed to elude him every time. "Aren't we?"

"It's all so messed up. You're my best friend. This was supposed to be your honeymoon with another woman. You were our best man, and that in itself to me screams *strictly* off limits. There's just so much…"

"Why don't you forget about what might be considered 'wrong', or what might look strange in the eyes of other people, Kelsey, and focus on how you feel. Does it feel wrong to *you*?"

"I don't know. I feel like I've lost you in some capacity."

"What? How?"

"It's hard for me to explain. But it's like you're gone as my friend now. And you're here as...something else, and I haven't gotten used to it yet."

He caught her face between his hands. "I will always be your friend. No matter what happens. I've abandoned you before. I'm never doing that again. I promise."

"Good, because let me warn you now, I can't go back to that," she said, tears welling in her eyes as she looked up at him. "Not seeing you or talking to you. It was more like hell than anything he put me through. I'm so scared of that happening again."

"I feel the same way. It won't. It won't happen again." He drew her face to his chest, stroking her hair and shushing her. Her arms tightened around him, but she seemed to relax into him everywhere else. And he whispered repeated nonsense meant to soothe her, though he knew it wouldn't. He'd hurt her, in his own way, just like Todd had. She shouldn't trust him any more than she did her ex-husband. All he could do was try to show her that he meant what he said. Show her every day from now on.

"Evan?"

"Hmm?"

"I'm sorry. Talk about ruining the mood."

"We'll get it back, honey." He nuzzled his mouth against the top of her head. "Soon as you spend the day like this, in my lovin' arms."

She grinned up at him, standing on her tiptoes for a kiss. "I think that'll do the trick."

"I don't know about you, but this is my idea of the perfect vacation," Evan murmured in Kelsey's ear that night, tracing her lower lip with the tip of his finger. "Eat, sleep, fuck, lie on the beach."

Kelsey gasped and giggled, snuggling closer to his warmth. It was an accurate description, blunt as it was. The rainstorm had battered the island most of the day, so they'd spent a majority of it cuddled in bed, napping, watching movies and ordering room service as the thunder rumbled and the rain poured down. Evan had even dragged her out on the lanai and they'd made out on the lounge, sprinkled with the cool splattering of raindrops blown in by the wind. Anyone who might have been watching wouldn't have seen much, but still it had been thrilling.

By the time it had cleared somewhat that evening, they'd been too zapped by their own inactivity to do much more than hang out on the sodden beach and eat some more. She'd probably gained ten pounds on this trip. Even so, if she were bound and forced to name a single day as her favorite of the entire vacation, this one would have to be near the top. Except for those few strange minutes in the kitchen, it was so much like old times…the dreary weekends they'd spent watching movies and generally being useless because there was nothing else to do. Or nothing else they wanted to do.

Now, there was the intimacy she'd always craved back then but could never have, the holding hands, the touches, the stolen kisses. It should have been paradise within paradise. Only paradise had a deadline, and it was approaching in a couple of days. They needed to talk, had to talk, and she had no idea how to instigate the conversation she prayed he would bring about himself: *what now?*

"This has probably been the craziest, scariest, sexiest, most emotionally exhausting and unbelievably orgasmic vacation I ever had," she admitted, taking a stab in the dark and hoping to hit her target.

He laughed. "Aw, sweetie, I meant to give you such a nice, relaxing time."

"This is better. Way, way better."

He traced his finger down over her chin. "Well, that orgasmic part? I'm about to bring that to the forefront. Again."

"Oh, God…"

So much for meaningful conversation. She wondered if, after that episode this morning, he only began making love to her to shut her up.

It was an effective technique and one she couldn't say she minded. He kissed her, a sweet, languid caressing of lips, his hands stroking down her bare back. She smoothed her palms over his chest, his shoulders, slipping her tongue into the rich flavor of his mouth as her nipples pebbled against his flesh. He groaned as his hand followed the curve of her hip and slipped into the crease of her bottom. His fingertips lined the cleft until he found her pooling moisture, and Kelsey's heart skittered. She snuggled closer to him as his erection slid against her thigh.

"See what you do to me?"

"Mmm, I like it," she whispered.

He slid his hand around to the front and urged her onto her back. "Open your legs."

She did.

"Wider."

"Evan…"

"Give me everything, baby girl, remember?"

He already had every part of her. The very nuclei of her cells cried out for him. She whimpered as two of his fingertips slid delectably over her clit, the too-light pressure urging her hips upward into his touch. And then he didn't have to coax her. She opened herself fully as his lips sought and found her nipple, locking around it with a gentle suction that had her arching her back and grasping his hair.

"If you keep doing that, I'm going to come."

His eyes flashed up at her. "Then come. It won't be the last time, I promise." He pushed his fingers into her pussy, and she felt her own wetness glide against them as her muscles clenched and she moaned.

"I love it when you make that sound," he said. "You only make it when part of me is inside you." He pushed deeper. "I love how you love this."

She nodded fiercely, scarcely able to breathe. "How could I not?"

His head slid down her belly, and anticipation exploded through her until she was squirming with need. Kelsey watched as he leaned over her and pressed his warm mouth against her mound, his fingers still buried deep and tight inside her. His tongue fluttered her throbbing bud and her breath became a burn through her lungs.

"Oooh, Evan."

He sucked her into his mouth and began slowly thrusting with his fingers, and then she couldn't open wide enough for him, couldn't get him deep enough, couldn't get enough of herself in his mouth. She sobbed and cried out and cursed until he made her come so hard she forgot her name, though she remembered his. Because she screamed it. And she collapsed, panting.

"You make me so fucking hard," he murmured as he slid up her limp body. She managed to reach down and touch him, her fingers tangling with his as he stroked himself. Maybe someday, when she could last a few minutes without jumping his bones at the sight of his nakedness, he would let her watch him do that until he came. A new rush of warmth throbbed between her thighs at the thought. But he was like a rock now, and she didn't want it anywhere but inside her. She gasped as the thick head nudged her wet entrance.

"Okay?"

"Sensitive."

"Mmm, I know. Just one more thing I love about you." He breached her, and she pulled tight and clung to him as enflamed tissues stretched and quivered around him. It was one long, slow slide that drove her out of her mind. She was aware of sounds coming from her lips but she didn't know if they were words or incoherence.

He paused and grasped her behind her knees, pulling both her legs over his shoulders. "More, baby, need more of you," he groaned in her ear.

"Then take all of me."

His breath rasped as he began to thrust, each stroke pushing farther, forcing the breath from her lungs, whimpers from her throat. "That's it. Oh, God, Kelsey."

She wished wildly in that moment for mirrored walls. She wanted to see it as she felt it and heard it, wanted to feast her eyes on the sight of his ass flexing as he thrust into her, wanted to see herself practically folded in half before him and taking his entire magnificent length. The thought of it alone had her teetering on the edge of climax. She reached up and grasped his face between her hands.

"Evan!"

His fingers slid over her clit, rubbing deliciously. "Are you going to come for me again?"

"Yes yes yes…"

"Jesus, you're perfect." He reached up and grasped the headboard, trapping her that way with her legs over his arms. Anchoring himself, he gave her everything. Hard and fast the way she wanted it. And his angle, oh God, it was hitting the right spot, wrenching a cry from her each time he brushed it. He smiled down at her in pure male triumph, adjusting his speed and depth so that he struck it again, over and over, and then she was lost in another orgasm so severe it didn't occur to her to do anything but grasp his hair and show him every way she could just how shattered she was. No hiding.

Somewhere in the middle of it, she felt him throb inside her, heard the growl tear from his throat, imagined him filling her up. It was sweet, so sweet, too sweet. It was something she wanted every night for the rest of her life. Him inside her. Leaving a part of him with her. She wanted to tell him she loved him so badly the words were like a monster in her chest trying to claw its way out.

They came down together, muscles relaxing and falling limp. Her knees slipped from his shoulders and she cradled his weight against her, stroking his sweat-slick back as he pressed gentle kisses to her lips, her cheeks. Her closed eyes. Gently, he withdrew from her and gathered her back into his arms, still prowling her body tenderly with one hand. She loved how he did that. It was so soothing after such a firestorm.

"It only keeps getting better," she whispered into his chest.

He smoothed his palm over the curve of her hip. "I know."

"It's scary to think that it can."

"That it can keep getting better? Why is that scary, baby?"

She paused before answering. "It just is."

And her heart ached, not with emptiness, but with the fullness he gave her. She was so confused. He'd promised to be her friend, to be there for her...but it wasn't enough. She'd learned long ago that as beautiful as her feelings for him were, they were nothing if he didn't feel the same.

The last thing she needed was another humiliation in her life. Which was the very thing she would be left with, if this didn't progress. If it went no further, if it ended. At least if it ended now, before they went home, the humiliation would be limited to their intimate circle of two. If they braved the questions from friends and family, and endured the likely outbreak of scandal they would cause back home, and *then* it ended… Hell, she would just have to move back to her hometown. Married the groom, had sex with the best man, and what next? Thank God Todd didn't have a brother the vicious tongue-waggers could link her with. She could hear it now.

And it would end, wouldn't it? She was sleeping with Evan Ross. She knew the consequences, knew the likely outcome, had seen it many times in the past, and still she'd done it. Why think she was any different than all the others? He claimed she'd been a fantasy of his and it had taken him ten years to realize it, but now that he'd had her, the mystique would wear off. Bumping their status from "friends" to "friends with benefits" was unacceptable to her now, even if there was a time she would have welcomed it, welcomed anything, any change.

She really could use a dose of his optimism right now, but his breathing was deepening and she wasn't sleepy at all. Sighing, she kissed his cheek and rolled from the bed, thinking she would walk out on the lanai and watch the waves for a while. Maybe some sudden wisdom would come from the sounds and the power of the ocean…or maybe sleep would come, at the very least. Their vacation would be over before she knew it, and she needed to get her circadian rhythms back on some semblance of a normal track.

She slipped into her robe and padded into the silence of the living room, heading toward the sliding glass doors. The sudden chirping of her cell phone lying on the coffee table made her jump mid-stride.

A call at 10:30 p.m. was usually nothing to get in an uproar over, but when she considered the fact that it was 2:30 a.m. back home, her heart skipped a beat. She scampered over to grab her phone and checked the display, shaken by the thought of Lisa or her baby having complications. The number was not one she recognized, but bore the familiar area code and prefix of Mannville, their home. She answered with a clipped, half-panicked "Hello?"

"Kelsey?"

It took her a moment to place the quivering female voice on the other end. When she did, ice flooded her veins. It was Todd's mother. "Sandra?"

"Honey, can you come to the hospital?"

Oh, God. "I'm out of town. Why? What's happened?"

"Todd has been in a car accident."

"Is he all right?"

"I don't *know* — " She broke into sobs for a moment while Kelsey concentrated on keeping her own heart beating, her blood flowing. She'd cursed the man, hated him for what he'd done to her, but she'd never wished for anything like this.

Though she supposed it had sounded that way when she'd screamed at him that she wished he were dead. For the past few months she'd tried to forget his face, but it was vivid in her mind then, so clear he could almost be standing in the room with her. Smiling, laughing, full of life. And he did have a beautiful smile, an infectious laugh. Those were the first things she'd noticed about him. His manner with her had always been gentle and loving until he'd turned indifferent and unconcerned. Until she'd stopped making him happy.

Oh, Todd, what's happened to you?

Sandra sniffled one last time and seemed to regain some of her usual composure. She'd lost her husband, Todd's stepfather, to an accident just five years ago. She must be so scared.

"He's still in surgery. He has internal bleeding. And I just...I'm all alone here."

She would be, Kelsey thought. Todd was an only child. Grandparents were dead. Sandra had brothers and sisters, but they were scattered across the country. She sounded like she was in shock. "Sandra, I would come in a heartbeat, but I…I'm…" *Out of town. Way, way out.*

"That's right, you said you were away. I'm sorry to bother you. I know things didn't end well with you and Todd, but honey, I know he still cares about you, and I still consider you part of this family."

"I know that. No matter what happened with us, I still care about him, too." She cast a glance toward the bedroom, where Evan lay sleeping. Did he share that sentiment?

It didn't matter. She didn't have it in her to turn down the woman who had been like another mother to her. And if Todd wasn't okay — it didn't bear thinking about — she had to get there. Had to tell him she was sorry for all the things she'd said, even if she told him as he lay unconscious.

"Sandra, I'll be there. But it'll take me… God. Hours." Enough to get a flight, fly eight hours, drive another two to get home from the airport. She could only pray that he would pull through, that she wouldn't be too late. "Is there no one else you can call to stay with you in the meantime? I'm worried about you. Can you call any of his friends, or" — she had to force herself to say the name — "Courtney?"

Sandra paused a moment, as if amazed Kelsey would make the suggestion. "I would, but I don't have any of their numbers. I don't know where Todd's cell phone would be, probably still in the wreckage."

Kelsey chewed her bottom lip and threw a glance at Evan's BlackBerry, resting on the bar that separated the kitchenette from the living room. Would he…? "Maybe I can get Courtney's. And she can call everyone else for you. Hold on."

She'd deleted all of Todd's contact numbers from her phone in a rush of fury long ago, even though she still had them in her head. Maybe Evan hadn't been so impulsive. She picked up his phone and went directly to the C's in his contact list, finding, sure enough, a slew of numbers for her. Boutique, home, cell, cabin... It was hard not to feel a twinge even as the information helped her at the moment. She recited Courtney's cell and home numbers through gritted teeth to Sandra, who thanked her profusely. But she had one more request, one that made Kelsey put a palm to her forehead.

"Do you think you can get hold of Evan for me? I really want to talk to him. The man who hit Todd was drunk. The police told me he's already *on* felony probation for drunk driving. He's in jail, and I want to make sure he stays there."

Kelsey glanced toward the bedroom again. "Yes, I think I know how to reach him."

"Good, good. You're still coming too?" she asked, fresh tears in her voice. "Please, Kelsey, if you can, I need you here. If he..."

"I'm sure he'll be fine. He has to be." What a happy reunion this would be. "I'll be at least twelve hours, but I'm coming."

They said their good-byes and well wishes. Still trying to squelch her tremors, she walked into the bedroom and rubbed Evan's bare arm where he lay on his stomach in bed. It was dark except for the dim light from the living room, but he must have sensed her distress somehow, either through her trembling hand or her rapid breathing. Or simply through being totally attuned to her, as he usually was. He lifted his head and squinted at her. "What's wrong?"

"I have to go home."

Evan managed to get them on a red-eye out of Honolulu. Kelsey, her hair up and her face scrubbed of makeup, took her seat and watched as he stowed their carry-on bags overhead. He hadn't had much to say since she woke him, and even now his face was grim, his jaw set. Not that she expected him to be overjoyed about this. She certainly wasn't.

"I'm sorry," she said, probably for the thousandth time, as he finished the chore and settled beside her.

"I told you, it's fine. You need to be there."

She sighed and pushed back in her seat, stretching her legs. They'd been sitting at the airport for what felt like hours, though it hadn't been that long. He'd told her again and again that he understood. But she knew if the situation were reversed—if it were Courtney's bedside he was rushing to— she could only imagine how it would feel. "I need to say it for the rest of my life, though. I've ruined your trip."

"It wasn't ruined, just cut short a couple of days. We'll make up for it someday."

Someday. It sounded too vague. Too distant, too undecided. She had a helpless feeling, like she'd touched heaven and was now watching it slowly recede from her sight. Fantasy had become her home for several days, and only upon leaving it was she realizing how safe and warm it had been. This plane would touch down in Reality. Cold and hard.

Kelsey took his hand, desperate for some reassurance, some comfort. He linked his fingers through hers. She'd been hoping for that response, but still it felt empty.

"He'll be okay," he said, giving her hand a gentle squeeze.

She hoped so with all her heart, but that hadn't been the assurance she was looking for from him. "I think so, too." She nodded, watching other passengers file in. It didn't look to be a full flight. "I mean, it's a pretty good sign they didn't have to airlift him, right? But I could tell Sandra is really scared. How was she when you talked to her?"

"Pretty much the same. And angry, too. But of course she would be, given what she's been through. She was practically like another mom to me growing up. It'll be good to see her again, just not under these circumstances."

Kelsey tore her absent gaze away from the vomit bag in the pocket in front of her—she hoped she wouldn't need it at some point—and looked at him. "You're going to the hospital with me?"

"Unless you don't want me there."

"Of course I do, I just…"

"Thought I didn't care?"

"No." Kelsey sighed miserably. "Courtney will probably be there, you know."

"I can deal with Courtney. Can you?"

"I suppose to avoid getting an assault charge in the hospital waiting room, I'll have to deal with her. Can't have you prosecuting me," she added in a lame attempt to lighten the mood.

He chuckled, then let go of her hand to pull his white cap low over his eyes and tilt his seat back. "Try to get some sleep."

"Yeah."

But she couldn't. She watched the lights slip by their window as they taxied. She breathed through the force pressing her back in her seat as they took off—she secretly hated to fly. Evan had kept her well entertained on the journey over, but now she was on her own. The ground fell away. The twinkling lights of Honolulu dropped from under them, growing more and more distant until there was nothing but the endless black void of the ocean below. How had things gone so horridly wrong over the space of a couple of hours? One minute Evan was making love to her, the next they were on a plane headed home and acting little better than strangers. Surely it was a bad dream, all of this. She would wake up in his arms any minute. Any minute now…

Her vision blurred and she shivered, wrapping her arms around herself until a flight attendant noticed and brought her a blanket.

It didn't help.

"You think I'm crazy, don't you?" Kelsey asked as Evan opened the glass door to Mannville Memorial's lobby for her. Even before they stepped over the threshold, that sterile hospital scent rushed out on a blast of air-conditioned air to swamp her. She didn't mind the smell so much when the visit was a happy one, like for the birth of a baby—and it looked as if she would get to visit Lisa in the hospital after all—but when a life hung in limbo, it was all the more stagnant and depressing.

"No, I think I am," he said. "God, this is going to be hard." They walked over to the elevator and he punched the button. Then he jammed his hands in his jeans pockets and stared at the floor.

They hadn't stopped since leaving the Houston airport, driving two hours straight to the hospital. She was dying for a shower and sleep. She'd been wide awake all through the flight. She'd watched the colors of dawn streak the sky, she'd watched the blessed ground finally rush up to meet them. The drive home had been spent mostly on the phone. She looked like hell and she was ready to drop. Last she'd heard, Todd had made it through surgery but wasn't out of the woods yet.

"Evan…"

"Yeah?"

Won't there be questions? Won't they see we came together and we both look like hell? What do we say? What is it that we have here?

She shook her head to clear out the thoughts and reached to put her arms around his waist. He pulled his hands out of his pockets and drew her to him, so she could feel him breathe. His chin rested on the top of her head. As close as they were standing, there seemed to be a gulf between them. It was a friend's hug. Not the intimate comfort between lovers who drew strength just from one another's embrace. But a pat-on-the-back, it'll-be-okay hug. *Please, God, let that all be in my head.* "Crazy as we might be, I am glad you're with me," she told him, trying to narrow the gap.

"Good," he said. "Because I feel like I really don't have a place here."

"Hey, I feel that way, too," she said gently. "But Sandra asked me to be here, that's all that matters. And I know she'll love to see you." She looked up at his face. The denim-blue shirt he was wearing dulled the intensity of his green eyes, making them appear almost murky. Or maybe it was just exhaustion. Her fault, all of it.

The elevator doors finally slid open, and she wasn't encouraged when he released her and stepped on, maintaining his distance once they were both shut inside.

It was then that she began to fume.

This was no picnic for her, either. She didn't want to be here, she wanted to be lying on the beach, or in bed with him, or stuffing her face with seafood. He lounged against the wall, watching the digital floor numbers tick by. She crossed her arms and stared at her feet. If this was the way it was going to be, she would play right along. For the last ten years of her life, she'd felt like she was chasing after love. First Evan's. Then Todd's when she realized something was wrong in their marriage. Now Evan's again. Damn him, he wasn't going to do this to her.

She bit her lip on a curse minutes later as they entered the fourth floor waiting area. Sandra was in the corner on the phone. A few of Todd's aunts and uncles and cousins were there, but Kelsey had never known them well—they were all from out of state.

Courtney's blonde head was bent over a magazine. That

hair… God, she would recognize it anywhere, without even seeing the face it framed. The strands twinkled as if tiny lights were embedded in them. She'd always envied that hair.

For a moment, she wanted to turn and bolt from the room. Or at least grab on to Evan. But he wasn't touching her, for support or otherwise.

Courtney's gaze flickered upward and tangled with hers. Kelsey saw her shoulders inflate with her breath, and slowly, she set her magazine aside. When her eyes moved to Evan, her expression flattened. Shattered.

Awkward.

"Kelsey!" Sandra had hung up the phone and was crossing the room, her arms outstretched. She caught Kelsey in a firm hug that belied her frail build. "I'm so glad you're here. It's so good to see you. Who's the handsome stranger you've brought with you?"

Evan grinned as Sandra moved to him, and he enfolded her in his arms. "Hey, beautiful."

"I've missed you both so much."

"I'm sorry," he told her, seeming unwilling to let her go. "I've been horrible. I'll come see you more often, I promise."

"Oh, honey, I know you're busy." Kelsey heard the unspoken words that filled the ensuing pause: *And I know my son wrecked your life.* "But you're welcome to come see me any time. Both of you." She withdrew from Evan's arms and dabbed at her eyes.

"Any change?" he asked.

"He's been awake, thank God," Sandra said, the weariness that only followed profound relief evident in her voice. "It looks like the surgery was a success."

"That's good."

Sandra looked them both over, puzzlement wrinkling her brow. "I'm almost more worried about you two right now. You both look exhausted. Where did you say you were?"

Oh, God. The question was aimed at Kelsey, who hadn't admitted where she'd been in any of her conversations with Sandra. It hadn't come up. Dammit, she and Evan should have discussed this! Desperately, she shot a glance at him. He was rubbing the back of his neck in an uncharacteristic fidget.

It wouldn't have mattered if they'd rehearsed what they were going to say or not. Evan wouldn't want to lie about it. She'd have felt guilty about making him. It was probably only her imagination, but it felt like every conversation in the room had dropped, and all eyes were on them. Especially Courtney's.

"We, uh...we were in Hawaii," Evan said, when it became apparent Kelsey couldn't get her voice to work.

"Oh." Sandra's gaze traveled between them, understanding dawning. Along with more than a little disappointment. "I had no idea. Kelsey, I'm sorry, honey, you should have told me. Of course I wouldn't have asked you to—"

"You were in *Hawaii*?" The hoarse demand came from behind Sandra, where Courtney had risen from her chair. Her blonde eyebrows pulled together in anguish, her fists clenched. "Evan, you took..."

She caught the words somehow, perhaps noticing how everyone swung to look at her, and leaned over to snatch her purse off the floor. It was then that Kelsey realized how the other woman looked; Courtney was always well put-together, immaculately dressed even when she was lounging around the house. But today she had on a plain red T-shirt and jeans that appeared to have come from the depths of the hamper. Kelsey stiffened as she stalked toward them, but she only swept past them and out of the waiting room. Evan watched her go, looking like he felt two inches tall. He even took a step toward the door as if he meant to follow her.

Sandra had a wounded look on her face, like a dream she'd long held precious had just been dashed on the rocks before her very eyes. Kelsey knew Sandra had always wished she and Todd would reconcile. Standing here with his family looking at her as if *she* had done something horrible, it was all too much.

"We only went so his trip wouldn't go to waste," she blurted. "We're just friends."

Todd's mother made a you-don't-have-to-explain gesture. Evan went utterly still, and the icy blast that blew up from the chasm between them was almost palpable. She didn't know what else he expected, given the way he'd been acting since leaving Hawaii. Was she actually supposed to stand here and announce they were together—when she had no idea if they really were—in front of Todd's entire family, who knew Evan so well, who even now were still casting her stunned, accusatory stares?

"You know what," Evan said, and when Kelsey looked at him, he was acting as if she wasn't even standing there, speaking to Sandra. "I think I'll stop by the PD and see if the offense report is ready on Todd's drunk driver. He was one of my defendants, anyway. I'll get his motion to revoke all worked up and ready to file first thing Monday morning."

"Evan, you don't have to do that. You look like you can hardly stand up," Sandra said.

"I'm fine. Really. I'll be glad to do it." His voice only said how much.

Kelsey crossed her arms and stared at her shoes. He was leaving her here. She felt like a lamb going to the slaughter. What a mistake this had been. This whole thing.

And now she was losing her best friend because of it.

No!

"Evan—" she began, unable to hide the note of desperation in her voice. He turned toward her, but his gaze focused somewhere around her throat, not her eyes. She stammered for a moment, her thoughts like scurrying mice.

"I... My stuff is still in your truck."

"I figured you'd be here a while. Do you need it right this minute?"

"Well..." *Shut up, girl, it'll be an excuse to talk to him later.* "No, I guess not."

"I don't know how late I'll be, so I'll drop it by my house. My brother will be there to let you get it."

"Oh. Okay. But, um, I'm kind of stranded up here—"

"I can give you a ride when you're ready," Sandra offered. Evan nodded, as if that sounded swell to him. He gave Sandra another hug and kissed her cheek, promising to keep her updated on what was happening with the case, giving his best wishes for Todd's swift recovery. To Kelsey, he only gave a brief nod before he left the room, left her, and was gone from her sight for the first time in nearly a week. Her heart feeling like a popped balloon in her chest, she dropped into a nearby chair and tried to hide her trembling hands from the watchful eyes of her ex-husband's family.

Chapter Ten

Just friends. We're just friends.

He'd uttered the same words just a couple of days ago to complete strangers on the dolphin tour, but it had been a joke. He'd made it so obvious that it was *only a joke*. Kelsey hadn't been teasing. She might have only been trying to save face in front of Todd's family, but that in itself grated his nerves until they were raw, naked wires under his flesh. Always it was about Todd fucking Jacobs. If she wasn't eaten up with guilt over not making him happy enough to keep his dick in his pants, she was crying over him, jetting off to be at his side when he got hurt. She was keeping her own feelings and happiness under wraps to remain squeaky-clean in the eyes of his family. Her life was still *consumed* with him.

And he didn't want any part of it until that man was exorcised for good…not by death, of course, but by *her*.

His legs ate up the distance down the hallway to the elevator, and he paced circles inside it after the doors closed. Hospitals had always smelled like pain and antiseptic and Band-Aids to him—God knew he spent enough time here talking to victims and their families—and Kelsey had traded tropical breezes and the scent of suntan lotion for this.

He tried not to be angry over that, he really did. He tried to understand. On some level, he did. Todd had been his best friend since they were toddlers. A year ago, Evan wouldn't have thought twice about this decision, he'd have been on the first plane. He might have anyway, if it hadn't been Todd who severed all contact between them. It hadn't been the other way around like most people believed. Evan would have listened to the man if he had something to say. He'd even called once and left Todd a voicemail, just to show he was open to communication. But the call back had never come, so as far as he was concerned, that was that.

It had been hard. Almost *thirty years'* worth of friendship gone, like it had never existed. It had been like losing a family member. The thought of something bad happening to his former friend had opened up a deep black hole in his chest. It had been scary as hell to wake up to news like that. He wanted him to be okay, but Evan's place wasn't here; he should have realized that sooner. Todd might not even want him here. Evan would make sure the guy who'd hurt Todd was behind bars for a good long time. That would be his contribution, though it was no less than what he would do for anyone.

It was all too complicated and he was too tired to try to sort it out. He just had to get away. Courtney floated through his chaotic thoughts, and he wondered whether he would have done the same thing for her. He still cared about her, but he hadn't been married to her. Never had uttered a vow before God and everyone to love and honor her till death. So he supposed it wasn't a fair comparison.

The elevator doors swept open and he strode out into the lobby. A flash of red caught his attention, and he saw Courtney standing in the little alcove where the vending machines were located. She was digging in her wallet for change.

He really should keep going and pray she didn't look over and see him, but something in her movements gave him pause. Her hands were shaking. When her change purse hit the floor a moment later, sending coins rolling every which way, she furiously shoved her hair behind her ear and knelt to retrieve it.

A quarter rolled on its edge to Evan's foot and he stepped on it. Her eyes went to him, and he saw her draw a breath before going back to her task. He bent to pick up her quarter and walked over to where she squatted, collecting others on his way.

"I got it," she mumbled as he reached her. She stood and he handed her the coins. But instead of buying a drink with them, she shoved it all back in her purse.

"Courtney."

"What?"

He shrugged and spread his hands. "I just feel like I need to say something to you. I don't know what. You have a way of making me feel like I need to apologize but I haven't done anything I need to apologize for, you know."

"I *know*. Look, I deserve everything I get, right?" Her eyes filled with tears. She hadn't been given to emotional displays when they were together. In fact, half the time he'd wondered what the hell was going on behind those cornflower blues. This had all started last Christmas. She couldn't get around him, couldn't talk to him, without acting this way. She was a mess.

"You deserve to be happy just as much as any of us. But I don't think you'll let yourself," he said.

"You could have told me you were taking another woman on our honeymoon."

He gave a sound that would have been a chuckle if there had been any humor in it. "It wasn't our honeymoon anymore. It was a trip to Hawaii, on my parents' money, that would have gone to waste if I hadn't used it."

"But to take *her* of all people, Evan—"

"She and I have been friends for ten years. Long before you and Todd came along, it was me and her. There was nothing wrong with us going away together." Even if it had turned into a total disaster.

"You're not *with* her, then?"

He thought of being *with* Kelsey. With her in the hot tub. With her in the shower. The bed. The couch. He thought of being buried deep inside her, coming with her, her breath on his neck, how sweet it had been every time. That sweetness hadn't dissipated as soon as he'd spent himself, either. It had lingered, a pleasurable haze in his thoughts, even through his sleep. It had been there to greet him when he opened his eyes in the morning to find her snuggled against him. He could feel no trace of it now. It was a world away. He was cold. "No."

She covered her face with her hands. "*God.*"

"What is it, Court? Come on, talk to me."

"I just want her out of my life."

"I'm sure she's had similar thoughts about you."

She pushed her hair back from her tear-stained face. Her blonde locks looked as if she hadn't brushed them since awakening to a frightening phone call. "I don't know if I can make you understand this. I really do love Todd. When I got the call that he'd been hurt, I think I realized just how much, because I thought of my life without him anywhere in it and…I couldn't breathe."

"Okay."

"I still care about you so much. I always will. A little part of me will always think I was crazy for messing up and not marrying you, because with you my life would have been secure and stable and…"

"Boring?" he supplied wryly.

"Not *boring*. Safe. Too safe, I think. But that doesn't mean

I particularly like hearing that my arch enemy is taking trips that *I* was supposed to take. I know it makes me a selfish bitch. I can't help it. It seems it's always about *her*. Every time Todd and I fight, it's about *her*. We split up because of *her*. And it just never stops."

"Trust me, I know the feeling." In fact, it made perfect sense to him. Which was only testament to how screwed up he was. He honestly thought he wouldn't notice if a Boeing 747 fell out of the sky and landed on his head at the moment. He certainly didn't think he'd care.

"But when it comes down to it, if you're not with her, then she's probably back here to nurse him back to health, and I'm sure he'd be all for it."

"I don't know. I don't have any answers. All I know is if the two of them decide to get back together, unhappy as they were, they both deserve whatever they get."

She stared at him, probably dismayed by his tone. Exhaustion was starting to overwhelm him, physically and emotionally. Caffeine was going to become a necessity if he wanted to get any work done. He reached out and put an arm around his ex-fiancée's quivering shoulders. "Come on. I'll buy you something in the coffee shop."

She nodded and let him lead her away.

From her hiding place around the corner, Kelsey drew a breath. She supposed she already deserved everything she got from this situation. But the words she'd said to Todd's mother couldn't have hurt Evan as much as that biting, bitter "no" he'd just uttered wounded her. She leaned against the wall to keep from collapsing into a boneless heap. Evan and Courtney were disappearing down a hallway now, his arm still around her.

Their being together right now didn't bother her as much as she'd thought it would. She doubted it was anything more than two hurting people reaching out to each other. Of course, things happened in those situations, as Kelsey and Evan had certainly proven this past week, but...surely not with them. Courtney had her chance. Evan didn't seem interested and if Courtney wanted Todd, loved Todd, she could damn sure have him. Kelsey certainly wasn't here to stand in her way.

She'd meant to make one last desperate attempt to catch Evan and explain her thoughtless words. But he obviously wasn't interested. She didn't think she'd ever heard him like that before. Not about *her*.

It was really over. And she couldn't face the family up on the fourth floor right now, not with her heart bleeding like a war wound. There was only one person she could think of to go to for solace, and Kelsey prayed they hadn't discharged her yet.

The maternity ward on the third floor was bustling with happy families and nurses in their bright-colored scrubs. Tiny baby wails drifted through the air. Kelsey stopped at the huge window looking into the nursery, where probably a dozen babies were lying in their cribs, some kicking and wriggling, some sleeping. Some wrapped in pink, some in blue. The name tag at the end of one read "Scott" in pink, and it was empty. A tired-looking nurse sitting at a computer at the nurse's station told her which room Lisa was in.

Kelsey's last remaining best friend was alone and propped up in bed, surrounded by flowers and balloons, cooing down at the pink bundle in her arms. She looked over when the door clicked shut. "Kelsey!"

"Hey, skinny. Oh, let me see." She made her way to the bed and leaned over to peek at a perfect little face, ignoring her friend's incredulous stare.

"Okay, I know you love me, but this is ridiculous."

"When are they letting you go home?"

"In the morning. I probably could have left today but I finagled another night until my mom gets here."

"Like you need help, Supermom."

"I don't need it, but I won't turn it down. Remember, Daniel lives in a state of panic during the newborn stage." Lisa snapped her fingers in Kelsey's face. "Hey. Look at me. Why are you *here*?"

Sighing, Kelsey turned away to drag a chair over to the bed. She dropped into it and rubbed her face hard with her hands. "I guess I blew it."

"What happened?"

"Todd had a wreck last night, a bad one. Sandra called and…"

Understanding slid across Lisa's expression. "Here you are."

"Here I am."

Lisa's head fell back on her pillow. "Oh, you moron. Buzz the nurse if my blood pressure skyrockets."

"It was a life-and-death situation and—"

"And what? You could somehow affect which way it went by being here?"

"Sandra asked me to come. She wanted me here. I'm far away from my own parents and she has *always* been there for me, like another mom."

"So you're here for her."

"Well, yes…"

Lisa's eyebrows lifted. "But?"

"I don't wish death on the man. I was with him for eight years of my life."

"And he didn't want you in his anymore, life, death or otherwise. So there."

Kelsey dropped her head in her hands and rubbed her temples. "I was hoping you'd help me feel better, not worse."

"You should have known better. Showing up in my damn hospital room when you should still be in Hawaii falling in love with a guy who I predict would *never* hurt you like that. I'm sorry if I sound coldhearted, but if Daniel had done to me what Todd did to you—"

"You don't know *how* you'd feel," Kelsey spat. "You've never been there."

Lisa leveled her with silent wrath in her gaze. "Fine. Is Todd all right?"

"He's been awake here and there. They're optimistic now."

"So what are you doing here? Go tell him you forgive him and beg him to take you back. Tell him you'll be his own Florence Nightingale to nurse him back to health."

"What? *No.* That's not what I want."

"Then you had better go tell that to Evan, and make him believe it, and pray he forgives you. God, Kelsey, I'm about to drop the 'f' bomb in front of my newborn daughter. And it'll be all your fault."

"It's pointless."

"You have to try. You have to bite the bullet on this one. This is your screw-up."

"I know. He said he understands. But I know he doesn't."

"Honey, he's a man. You just trounced all over his ego, and after he's spent all week marking his territory, his territory suddenly up and flew back to the mutt it belonged to before. You have to do whatever it takes to *let this go*, or you and Evan will never make it. You'll never make it with anyone."

Kelsey nodded, picking at her fingernails. "I know," she said again. She dared a glance at her friend, whose brow was furrowed in concern. Lisa's blonde hair was pinned up and she hadn't a speck of makeup on. She supposed they both looked the same, except Lisa wasn't wearing the physical manifestations of emotional turmoil on her face. "You look great," Kelsey told her. "Really. You look happy."

"Quit trying to butter me up. Come here, you." Lisa held one arm out and Kelsey went in for the hug, careful not to jostle Meagan. "I suggest you try 'happy' for a change, okay?" Kelsey nodded against her shoulder as Lisa patted her back. "It'll be okay, hon."

"You've got this mom thing down, that's for sure," Kelsey laughed, pulling back. She wiped her eyes. "We got a ton of stuff for her, but it's all in Evan's truck." Her heart twisted into a painful knot at the memory of how much fun they'd had together picking out the clothes and toys. It seemed like a lifetime ago, though it had only been a couple of days.

"Well, there's your perfect excuse."

"No, he said he'd leave it all at his house and his brother would let me in to get it. He's working late tonight, I guess." *Or he could be consoling Courtney all night, you know.* Reminiscing over coffee turns into an outpouring of regrets turns into her crying in his arms... It seemed the more time went by, the more those thoughts crept in. Began to take hold and turn her vision red.

"I just don't find that acceptable," Lisa said. "Do you?"

Kelsey shrugged. The aching knot of her heart had just spun in place at the thought of facing him. "I don't want to bother him right now. He needs to cool off. You should have seen him. He wouldn't even look at me."

"Quit backing down. You were *so close*. Isn't he worth fighting for?"

He was. He was so worth it. And she was so, so scared. "Worth getting my heart splattered all over hell just like all the others before me?"

Lisa didn't reply, only sighed heavily. Kelsey forced a smile and nodded toward Meagan dozing in her mother's arms. "Now, if we're done with all that, I really need to hold that baby, if you don't mind."

"Of course. Baby therapy always helps."

She tried to shove all thoughts aside as Lisa put Meagan into her arms, but found it wasn't easy. Newborns always enamored her, from their little wrinkled fingers to unbelievably tiny toes. She could have sat forever holding her. Meagan already had her mother's lips and just a tuft of her dad's brown hair. Kelsey smoothed it down, imagining if Evan ever had kids, they'd all have hair just like his—so thick and black it seemed genetically inescapable. Hopefully, they'd be blessed with his green eyes as well. If only she could be lucky enough to be their mom, then maybe that hair would have a bit of unruly curl, and those eyes would have a roundness that somewhat softened the piercing intensity of their color…

Lisa napped for a bit, and Kelsey took the opportunity to shed the tears she'd been holding back as she stared down into the baby's tiny sleeping face. Watching her yawn, smack her little lips, wrap her tiny fingers around Kelsey's own with a surprisingly firm grip. *Try happy for a change.*

When she'd said her wedding vows, she'd taken them seriously, and she'd meant them to last forever. She never would have broken them. That was part of the pain of it all. Todd hadn't felt the same way. So she was adrift, for some reason feeling bound by words to a man who had cut her ruthlessly from his life. Even being with Evan this week, heavenly as it had been, had felt like a betrayal. Wrong. Not because of any lingering love she felt for Todd, but some twisted sense of faithfulness.

That wasn't twenty-first century thinking, but it was the values she'd been raised with.

Lisa was right. Evan was right. Her own heart was right. She couldn't keep going on like this. Values or no, she had to start letting go. Start standing up for what she wanted.

"Always listen to your mom, little girl. She gives good advice, even if it hurts to hear." Meagan cracked open one blue eye to gaze up at her and gave a tiny cry of agreement.

God knew she was ready for a change. And some happiness.

Kelsey's scent still lingered in his truck. Evan slammed the door and gripped the steering wheel until his knuckles were white, fighting himself. He really should go in and get her; he shouldn't have left her like that. He'd promised not to abandon her again and he'd done just that. But this was where she wanted to be, or else they would still be in Hawaii right now. He would call her later, try to sew his heart back together and continue being there for her no matter what, like he'd told her. It would be the hardest thing he'd ever done in his entire life.

He sat in silence while it seemed all hell raged inside his head. It hurt. God, it hurt. More than it had when Courtney betrayed him, more than it had ever hurt when a relationship ended. He'd usually been the one ending them, anyway. Kelsey had been like his lifeline through all of that. His one hope, his only assurance that maybe there was someone else like her out there. That maybe that elusive *she* really existed, just waiting for him to find her.

It had been her all along.

If that was the case, then bachelorhood for life was looking pretty appealing right now. He would learn to listen to his damn head one day. The one that could pick apart the most intricate details of a case, argue them and win. Not the one that kept screwing up his life.

He'd wanted to tell Courtney that if she truly loved Todd she needed to fight for him, and may the best woman win. But somehow that seemed like a betrayal of Kelsey. If Todd was who she wanted, if he was who would make her happy, Evan didn't want to sabotage that for her. Maybe Todd had learned his lesson and they would work it out this time. Have their happily ever after. But they'd do it without Evan anywhere near their white-picket-fence-two-point-three-kids American dream.

Of course, that would mean going back on his promise to her. Shit.

Taking a deep breath, he started his truck and busied himself adjusting the mirrors, though they were fine already. Work. He would throw himself into work, his old defense mechanism, always there for him when his personal life was in shambles. There would be a ton of it waiting for him. He could spend most of the weekend at the office if he had to, just to keep his mind off her.

He only hoped she wouldn't prove to be a force too powerful to shove away with indictments and motions and graphic offense reports.

She'd told Evan she couldn't deal with losing him, but Evan had always been the one telling her she could deal with anything. It was time to prove him right.

Once she'd expended the benefits of kitty therapy that weekend, Kelsey ambled through her bedroom, past the luggage she hadn't yet opened, and to her closet. It was past noon on Saturday and she was still in her pajamas with her hair half-falling from a sloppy bun. She planned on staying that way. There was work to do, and probably a lot of tears to shed, if her supply wasn't already depleted. Lisa was busy with her new baby. Kelsey's mom and dad were on vacation themselves. No one she knew needed to listen to her weeping and whining right now. She was on her own.

The box on her closet's top shelf hadn't been disturbed

since she'd shoved it there months ago upon moving in. She'd thrown out a lot of artifacts and reminders from her marriage—most of them, actually—some during fits of blind rage. But even then, the mementos in this box alone had remained untouched, because they were the most precious to her. She finally understood why.

As she slid the cardboard box down from its safe place while her cats swirled around her ankles, her mouth was dry and her pulse throbbed. She carried it to her bed and settled herself cross-legged on the mattress, thinking she probably needed a box of Kleenex before she got started. But what was the point? She was home, she was alone, no one would be knocking on her door. Evan's solitary text message early this morning asking if everything was okay was proof that he was in no hurry to speak to her, especially since he hadn't responded to her reply. He was merely trying to assuage the sense of obligation he felt to her, to their friendship. He'd promised he would always be there for her. But he wouldn't be there in the capacity she needed him, not unless she made some changes.

And even if he would *never* be there—a thought that made a panicky fullness rise in her chest—this was something she had to do for herself.

Inside the box were letters, pictures, printouts of e-mails... She dug deeper, finding her old college journal and a scrapbook. There were silly things like a napkin from a restaurant she and Todd had eaten at on their honeymoon. A couple of stuffed animals he'd given her. Typical fossils of a long-dead relationship. But she began to detect the pattern she'd suspected all along.

All of the letters and e-mails had been sent while she was still in college and Todd was back home waiting for her to graduate. She picked up the very first one her fingers brushed—a printout of an e-mail he'd sent her—and began to read it.

I just got off the phone with you two hours ago but I can't stop thinking about you. I would call you again, but I'm afraid you're asleep by now. I'm also afraid I'm going to go crazy before I get to see you again...

And more of the same from all the others:

Yesterday was so amazing. It's hard to believe I'm back here now away from you. I have to look at your picture a dozen times just to get through the day, Kelsey. I can't wait until we can be together every day. I'm counting the days.

"Ugh, sappy bastard," she grumbled. Taking a deep breath, she furiously wadded each letter into a tight little ball. It was as she'd suspected. She'd been in love with the way Todd made her feel about herself. Evan had been her best friend, but his treatment of her, in a way, had been a rejection. Every single day for two damn years, she'd felt rejected by him. It was no wonder her self-esteem had been so beaten down she'd fallen for the first sweet-talker to come along.

The whole box had to go, but she made a point to look at each thing inside it and remember why she'd kept it. After that, it went back in the box bound for the Hefty bag waiting in the kitchen.

Except for one thing: her journal. Throughout all the letters and photographs, she'd shed not one tear until she opened the little book and began to read. A couple of hours later she was halfway through it, and she was a sopping wet mess her cats regarded with concern.

When it felt as if the walls were about to close in on her, she took a break, dug her bikini out of her suitcase and headed down to sit by the pool. It was empty except for a few kids and evening swimmers. One of them was the guy down the hall who had asked her out about two months ago. She'd taken the chicken way out and claimed one excuse after another until he finally got the hint. He seemed nice enough, fairly good-looking. The kind of guy she might have eventually gone out with, when she was ready. But there were no sparks there. Evan's words floated through her mind: *Doomed to contentment.*

That's what she wanted—no, that's what she wanted *desperately*—to avoid. If a guy couldn't do to her body the things Evan had done mere days ago, if he couldn't send scores of chills up her arm just by brushing it, make her wet just by letting his gaze wander down to her breasts, she had no use for him. Evan had ruined her for anyone else, damn him. He was going to have to reap the consequences of that.

Phase One of her plan was over. Phase Two she would tackle tomorrow. God give her strength.

Todd was wrapped almost from head to toe, but Kelsey would lay bets he didn't feel much worse than she did at the moment. His entire right leg was in a cast, as well as his left wrist. His head was bandaged and the left side of his face was purple. Thank God she hadn't run into his mom or Courtney on her trek to his room, but they were lurking somewhere, she was sure. She had to make this as quick and painless as possible.

"Hey," he said—it was more like a croak—and there was as much surprise in his voice as she figured he could muster.

"I'm not going to ask how you feel. I imagine that's a pretty stupid question right about now." He grunted some response that might have been a laugh if he hadn't recently had surgery on his ribs. "They say you're going to be just fine."

His gaze followed her as she approached the side of his bed. "Yeah, it doesn't feel like it sometimes. You look tired."

You have no idea. "I'm all right."

Todd was silent for a moment. She couldn't see enough of his face to discern what emotions might be crossing it. "My mom told me that when she called you, you were in Hawaii with Evan," he said.

Good. He'd had time to prepare. She'd been afraid Sandra wouldn't tell him. "I was."

"Are you and he…?"

"He invited me, and I went, it's pretty much as simple as that. Or it started out that way, at least. It was the trip he should've taken with Courtney, as their honeymoon. But that didn't work out, did it?"

It was hard not to look away from him as she uttered those words, but she forced herself to keep her gaze fixed on him. To not retreat from what she had to tell him. She looked him up and down and felt…well, *nothing* was too harsh a word. There was sorrow at seeing such a strong man in a nearly helpless state. But he would heal over time. Lisa's words about begging him to take her back floated through her mind. That was, indeed, the absolute last thing she wanted in the world, especially after the beauty of last week. It would be like tasting Rocky Road ice cream for the first time after only knowing plain vanilla, only to be told she had to go back to vanilla from now on. The vileness of her reaction to that thought seemed to give her the strength she needed.

"But whatever happens with Evan and me, I—I have very strong feelings for him, yet I basically left him to come here. I've been asking myself why. You made it quite clear you didn't want me in your life, but I've possibly ruined something wonderful over you. Why would I do that?"

"I didn't crash my truck into that idiot on purpose to make you feel bad, you know. It's not always about you—"

"I'm going to stop you right there, because I heard a lot of BS from you for weeks after we split, and now I have you where you can't run from what I have to say, don't I?" Surprise rounded his brown eyes. "But I'm sure the doctors wouldn't want me getting you upset. I'm not here to do that, and I hope you understand. I'm done with yelling and screaming at you about how you ripped my heart out and turned my life upside down, and you've heard it all before anyway. I'm just going to tell you that you've done it for the last time. You've had some kind of sick hold on me ever since what you did, and now I hear—whether it's true or not—that you might actually *miss* me."

"I know what I did to you was wrong. I just feel like I need to make it up to you somehow."

"That's just guilt talking. I know I said some things that have probably stuck with you all this time, if you have a heart at all. You can forget all that, it was just my own anger and pain and frustration talking, wanting to hurt you like you'd hurt me. The problem was, I couldn't do it, because you simply didn't care. If we got back together you know as well as I the same thing would just happen again."

"I wouldn't—"

"I would never be able to make myself believe whatever you're about to say. There was a time when I was pathetic and weak and desperate and I might've given us another chance, but no more. *No more*. I'm going to walk out the door, find Evan and try to be worthy of him. I'm afraid it's too late, but at least I don't have your shadow hanging over me anymore."

His throat constricted as he swallowed, and it seemed to pain him. Her natural wifely instinct was to move toward him, try to make him more comfortable, ask if he needed anything. But she stood her ground. He was fine. She had to keep telling herself that. He would be fine, she would be fine, everything would be fine.

For a moment she thought he wasn't going to reply, but when he did, it momentarily stunned her. "He's a good guy."

She nodded. "He's the best of us all. He was at his office

on his vacation just to be sure the motion to revoke gets filed as soon as possible on the guy who hit you."

Todd swallowed again, and she wondered if that glistening in his eye might've actually been a *tear*. God forbid he showed any emotion. "I miss him. Wish I could see him. Will you... tell him I'm sorry? And thank him for everything he's done?"

Her heart softened. He sounded more genuine talking about Evan than he ever had talking about her. "Of course I will. But I don't know if it'll do any good."

"I know. Courtney and I...we're not together anymore, you know. She's here and she's hardly left my side, but...I don't know."

"I imagine you'll work it out. You should, anyway. You seem well suited for one another. She loves you, but I think you two can't really see one another without your guilt getting in the way. You need to get rid of it."

Todd's jaw flexed in a smile. She could tell from his drooping eyelids he was getting sleepy. Probably pain meds kicking in. "I'll work on it."

"Good." She adjusted her purse strap on her shoulder. "I should get going. I wish you the best in everything, Todd."

"You, too. Kelsey? You look beautiful."

She gaped for a moment. For all his praise in the beginning of their relationship, she'd hardly heard those words throughout their marriage. "You *did* take quite a hit on the head, didn't you?"

"Yeah, I think it knocked some sense into me."

She laughed, moving toward the door. "Well, let's hope that's the case."

And as luck would have it—*her* luck lately, at least—she came face-to-face with Courtney in the hall outside the elevator. She almost had to chuckle at the way Courtney's eyes rounded and her body seemed to go on full alert, as if anticipating a physical attack. The Styrofoam coffee cup in her hand shook visibly.

A few months ago, she might've had cause to worry. For the first time since finding the other woman in bed with her husband, Kelsey offered her a big smile. She swept her arm in the direction of Todd's hospital room.

"He's all yours."

Chapter Eleven

Evan burst through his office door like a whirlwind, tossing down his briefcase and shedding the jacket that was stifling him. It took every ounce of self-control he could muster not to slam the door behind him, but that might incite a parade of staff members asking if everything was all right. They were a close-knit bunch, sometimes too much so. He'd already been an ass to his assistant this morning, prompting her to ask him if he needed another week off. He only wanted to start the previous one over. The good parts, at least.

Finally in the silence and solitude of his office, he took a breath and stared at the bleak scene beyond his tall, narrow second-floor windows. Rain drooled down the glass, and the sky was leaden and dismally gray. Matched his thoughts perfectly. It was one of those days he'd told Kelsey about, when it had taken everything he had to walk into that courtroom.

Today was shaping up to be a nightmare, and he didn't know if the judge was really riding his ass that hard or if it was just that he was ready to snap. Or if it was that Kelsey had been sitting across the room, the weight of her gaze following his every move.

Normally her court attire was conservative and demure and, while nothing she was wearing today was revealing at all, something about the way her black skirt clung to her ass had his blood boiling. Whenever she walked up to the court clerk, he wanted to jump up and thrash every bastard in the room for daring to watch her.

But how could he blame them? Her skirt, her pumps accentuating every muscle in her calves, her hair cascading in gorgeous spirals down her back... A man would've been out of his mind not to look. And he could swear the bewitching glow of a woman well fucked still lingered in her face. She looked amazing while he had hardly slept for two days and it showed. The judge had probably taken one look at the dark smudges under his eyes and concluded he'd been on a bender all weekend. This wasn't how his fantasy was supposed to play out, not at all.

He'd wanted to call her. The thought of her at the hospital, sitting at Todd's bedside holding his hand, had stopped him dead. That man had already made a fool of him once and he'd be damned before he'd willingly go and let him do it again.

His desk phone gave a shrill chirp, slicing through the tumult of his thoughts. He should've told Delilah to hold his calls. Court didn't resume for another two hours and he needed them to recuperate. He was off his game. Dammit, he was *never* off his game.

Dropping heavily into his chair, he stabbed the intercom button. "Yeah."

"Kelsey's here to see you."

Fuck. The last thing he needed was her in here spewing apologies or excuses or whatever she had in mind. He crammed the heels of his hands into his eyes, fighting the urge to growl out loud.

"Evan?"

"Send her in."

He sounds horrible.

Kelsey watched as Delilah frowned down at the phone on her desk. "I really don't know what's gotten into him today. After a week in Hawaii, you'd think he'd have mellowed out."

"Withdrawals, maybe," Kelsey said, striving for cheerfulness. "I mean, you get a week on the beach and then you have to come back to this place on a rainy Monday? That would give anyone the *blah*s."

Delilah nodded and laughed, then leaned forward conspiratorially, speaking in hushed tones. "Hey, *you* would know. Who did he go with? We've decided it was a woman because he never would say."

God, she should have suspected the tongues were wagging. Delilah's, especially. She was the gossip of the courthouse, on top of all the scandals. Kelsey feigned innocence, cocking her head to one side as if contemplating the matter. Hopefully none of the DA's staff knew Kelsey had been off last week, too, or they might put two and two together. But did she really care anymore? "Hmm, must be really top secret."

"Must be, if he didn't tell you. Anyway, you can go on back. You know where his office is, right?"

"Yeah."

Left on her own again, her courage nearly failed her. If he still maintained that *distance*, she didn't know what she would do. Oh, God. What if she could never bridge it? What if that terrible politeness—or if this morning was any indication, outright hostility—would be the extent of their relationship from now on? She clutched the file she was carrying to her chest like a shield as she navigated the hallways.

His office was down the first hall to the right, second

door on the left, and it was closed. Holding her breath, she tapped on it, bracing herself for a brusque reply. But Evan only sounded defeated when he mumbled for her to come in.

It crushed her. Her easy-going, roll-with-it Evan had been replaced with a man who looked tense and unhappy, and it was her fault. She slipped inside the door to find him at his desk, every iota of his attention focused on the laptop in front of him. The glare of it caught in his reading glasses, and for all his brooding, he was sexy as hell. She doubted there was anything on that screen that had him looking so intense. He was just avoiding meeting her eyes. She closed the door behind her.

"Hi," she said. Finally he raised his head, and she would have been relieved when he smiled, but it looked forced. Like everything else about him.

"Hey, there. Did Jack send you over to gloat about his petty victories?" He winked as he said it, but it was true that he'd had a hard morning. The judge had shot down almost every objection he'd thrown out there, and as time pressed on Evan's frustration had been evident. But she'd seem him handle far, far worse than that, had seen him shake it off like it was nothing and laugh about it later.

Standing here now, she couldn't quite get rid of the ridiculous feeling that he was the authority figure behind his massive, imposing desk, and she the shamed underling pleading her case. *No begging*, she ordered herself. *Have some damn dignity*. "No, of course not," she said. "I wanted to see you."

She stepped farther inside the room, feeling self-conscious despite herself as his gaze swept her up and down. Of all times, she thought about the naughty things he'd said about having sex in here, and her cheeks began to heat up. "I'm sorry for what I said at the hospital. I wasn't prepared to answer questions about us yet. It's all so new. And we haven't exactly discussed where this is going."

He pulled off his glasses and tossed them on the desk. "I thought it was pretty damn apparent where it was going."

"*It* went to the bedroom. I didn't know if *it* was coming home with us, or if it was a 'what happens in Waikiki…' thing." His office was spacious, and neat as always. His law degree was elaborately matted and framed on the wall behind him. Pictures of his family adorned the shelves. It struck her then, perhaps more than ever before, just how much she wanted to be a fixture in his world. The wound in her heart yawned wide at the thought that she'd utterly mucked up her chance. "After what happened to me, I need something concrete. I need it laid out in black and white what's going on, because I'm not going to take the risk of sparking off yet another scandal in my life by speculating in front of a roomful of people. Can you understand that?"

"All right, we should've talked openly about it. Point taken. But I wasn't too keen on making any declarations of love and devotion while you're obviously still upset about your ex."

Love?

"No, no," she said, trying to hide her desperation as she dropped into the chair on the other side of the desk from him. She had to make him understand. "I'm not upset about him."

"The opposite of love is indifference, and you're not indifferent to Todd. You're still mad as hell."

"Mad at what he did to me, to my life. I saw him yesterday, and I feel nothing whatsoever for him, even when he's lying broken in that hospital bed. I hope he heals, I wish him the best, but…honestly, you have to believe me. I'm putting it all behind me. I told him that."

"You did? You said those exact words?"

"I told him this was the last time he would cause me heartache or turn my life upside down. I guess I just needed to get those words out, you know? I needed closure. I never could get it before." She looked him in the eyes. "He knows where you and I have been. He wanted you to know he misses you, and wanted me to thank you for everything you've done. It felt pretty damn good, getting all that out there. Like I'm finally free."

"Then I'm proud of you," he said, sincerity in the words. His expression had softened when she told him what Todd said about him. But his smile didn't quite reach his eyes.

"Do you not believe me?" she asked miserably.

"I just don't think it's been put to the test yet." He sighed. "What happens the next time we're away and he needs you for whatever reason?"

"Nothing. I told you Sandra—"

"I *know* what you told me, but is Sandra really the reason you flew three thousand miles to be here when he got hurt? Or was it that you got scared and jumped at the first opportunity to run away from me and back to the familiar?"

She just stared at him. It was probably the closest thing to the truth in existence, insane as it sounded, and she hadn't even thought of it herself.

He went on. "I didn't mean to scare you. And I want Todd to be all right, don't get me wrong. I'm trying not to be a jealous asshole about it. But I did lose one girl to the guy and this... It wasn't cool. It exacerbated all this other stuff I've been stewing over all week."

"Like what?" she asked in a tiny voice.

His mouth twisted, as if words were pressing in behind it and he was trying to rein them in. "All those tears you shed over him. It's bothered me from the first night we were together."

Her brows drew together and she shook her head. "Evan, those were for *you*. For the feelings you were showing me that I'd never felt before. For all the years I wanted you and never thought I would have you." Her eyes were welling even at the mention of it.

He looked as if his world had just spun. "What?"

"How could you honestly *not know*?" Drawing a deep breath, she reached into her manila file and pulled out the two sheets of paper she'd copied at the office that morning. She stood and dropped them on the desk in front of him, emotions threatening to sweep her away at what she was doing: showing him the confession forever captured in her teardrop-splattered handwriting on those pages. It was everything she'd ever wanted to say to him and never had the guts to. "There. There is my heart laid open for you, okay? I wrote this in my journal one night back in college, and after last week I know that not a word on those pages has changed. So read it, and if it isn't proof enough of how I feel about you, and if you can't forgive me for one hasty decision, maybe it's best we're over before we ever really began."

He stared down at what she'd written, but she couldn't tell if he actually read the words. "Look, I knew, but I didn't know you felt like *that*. That deeply."

"Now you have it in black and white." She was shaking all over, tears streaking her cheeks. When had she walked around his desk to stand beside his chair? Her heart was threatening to choke her. Taking a breath, she straightened and smoothed her damp palms on her skirt. *Dignity, right.* He probably thought she was an insane stalker now.

"If I humiliated you, I'm sorry, but I was a walking pile of humiliation over you for two years until I met Todd, and he managed to pick me up somewhat before slamming me right back down. That will *never* happen to me again. I told Todd he couldn't hurt me anymore, and now I'm telling *you* that if you want me, get off your ass, because I love you, Evan, more than anything"—she paused to sob, those words wrenching her soul—"but I refuse to live like this anymore."

He cleared his throat and lifted his gaze to hers. "I have so much to say to all that it'll take the rest of the day to get it out." He glanced down at her journal entry, at the words that had flown from her hands the night she'd watched him with the girl at the frat party. She'd wanted to be that girl so desperately she might have sold her soul for it that night. "But since we're a little strapped for time, consider this me… getting off my ass."

He stood, and she had no time to brace herself before he jerked her to him and scalded her lips with his own. She shook, went limp and groaned helplessly against the onslaught, disbelief fogging her senses along with a desire so strong she could scarcely contain it.

He was real and solid and hot in her arms, burning her even through all their layers of clothing. Layers she couldn't wait to strip through. She clenched his shirt in her fists, feeling his back muscles tense beneath her fingers, feeling his thigh surge hard between hers until her skirt rode up her legs, higher and higher until he must have felt he heat of her pussy through his pants. The edge of his desk bit into the flesh of her ass as he planted her against it.

"I need to lock my door," he murmured, his lips scarcely leaving hers as he spoke.

"I did it when I came in."

"So certain of your powers of persuasion?"

"Something like that."

Breathing labored, Evan grasped the lapels of her jacket and stripped it down her arms. When she moved to help him remove it completely, he held it just at her forearms, trapping both limbs useless behind her back. He pulled away to look at her and when she lunged forward to claim his mouth, he eluded her, holding her still.

"Please," she whispered.

"You said you loved me."

"I do, I love you." It rolled so naturally off her tongue now, as if she had been saying it all along. It didn't even matter if he said it back. "I swear to you, if it had been you who got hurt, I couldn't have even waited for a flight. I'd have swum the ocean to get to you."

"Remember when you asked me what makes me hurt?"

She nodded. "Of course."

"You know the party when I first introduced you to Todd?"

"Yes."

"I have a confession, too. I was waiting for you to show up there because I'd made up my mind that I'd messed around long enough and I wanted to be with you. I knew, even back then, that you and me would be forever. As a twenty-two-year-old that scared the hell out of me, until I realized the thought of you not being there after graduation scared me far more."

Her trembling intensified. He was going on. "I only made the mistake of introducing you to my best friend before I could take you away to tell you this. And I saw you guys stare at one another a little too long, and then you talked all night and finally left together. I decided maybe it was a sign we really weren't meant to be. It was the only consolation I could find."

"Evan…"

He shushed her with a finger to her lips. "Let me say this. The one thing I'm thankful for is that being with him kept you in my life all these years. But I can't forgive myself for not giving us a chance sooner. I was always in one meaningless relationship or another and none of them were worth hurting you like that."

"It's okay. If it ends with us here, like this, it's all okay."

"Nothing is ending here." He kissed her, as she'd been dying for him to do. Emotionally, she was numb, in shock, but her physical need for him hadn't suffered. It eclipsed all other thought.

The finger he'd pressed to her lips had trailed down over her chin, following the hollow of her throat to the V-neck of her teal blouse. She panted, wanting to thrust her breast into his hand, but his fingers busied themselves deftly working her buttons. She wiggled her hips closer to him, needing more contact. He tasted so heavenly she couldn't get enough of his lips, of the teasing way his tongue swirled with hers.

Cool air caressed her breasts when he freed her shoulders of her blouse and her bra straps, and it was unbelievable to her that she was actually bare-chested in the workplace. Dear God, she'd never been so wanton. A mere month ago, the very thought would have mortified her. But Evan's lips slipped over her nipple and there was no room for anything except raw sensation. Still trapped and helpless, she ached to touch him, to clench his silken hair in her fingers. He licked and sucked until she was as wet between her legs as the flesh he kissed, her hips undulating to his rhythm.

His hand trailed up her thigh, under her skirt, to grasp her panties and give them a sharp tug. She moaned and shifted to help him pull them all the way down, feeling them slip off over first one high heel and then the other. His fingertips brushed over her clit and she melted in agony as he rubbed. "Mmm. God, I can't wait to get you home," he murmured.

She giggled. "I thought you wanted to do it here?"

"Oh, we will. But to have you naked in my bed…at *home*. It'll just seem more real. More permanent."

Permanent. Had a single word ever sounded more beautiful to her?

He pulled her away from the desk then and wrenched her jacket off, his movements now nearly uncontrolled. Arms finally free, she clutched at him in relief. With both hands, he pushed her skirt so far up her legs she was naked from the waist down.

"I've wanted to do that all morning," he said, before lifting her and setting her precariously on the edge again, spreading her legs to accommodate his hips. She was so eager to feel him wedge into her she was dripping, panting, her pulse frantic. But he dropped to his knees.

How could she have ever lived the rest of her life without this? She cried out when his tongue speared her, lapping at the cream she wept just for him, just from his nearness, his touch. He groaned and her face burned but she was beyond embarrassment. God knew he'd seen every bare inch of her in every position imaginable over the past few days. She'd gone through too many emotions today, and now that it was over she wanted him to fuck her until she was numb. But he wouldn't lick her in a rhythm that would bring her any relief, and she was caught at the precipice of ecstasy, writhing against him.

She murmured in frustration when his mouth abandoned her. He stood, one hand wrenching at his pants as the other anchored her around the waist. "Kelsey," he whispered against her ear, and moments later she felt the broad head of his cock nudge her opening. Her heart dropped as he pushed into her in that overpowering way of his, holding her tight.

She gasped his name as he cursed and filled her in every capacity, physically and emotionally. A leftover tear dripped from her eye, splattering on his shoulder.

"Shhh," he whispered, stilling his movements. His cheek grazed hers, deliciously coarse with a hint of stubble, as he sought the corner of her lips with his. "I love you."

"Oh, God." She lifted her head to meet his kiss, joy and elation flooding her along with the fear that could only come with getting the one thing she'd wanted for so long. She wouldn't let it go this time. "I love you."

"Baby, I'm sorry."

He reached up to wipe her tears away and she let him for a few moments, until his scrutiny became too much and she pitched herself into his arms. Gently, he withdrew from her almost all the way before guiding himself back into her desperate heat. Her body readily welcomed him as his lips explored the wetness on her cheek.

"These tears are all for me…" he murmured, sliding his hands beneath her bottom to hold her still as he took her with gentle thrusts.

She couldn't form a reply at the moment; her throat muscles were locked around her moans of ecstasy. Those deep, slow strokes were driving her out of her mind. After just a couple of days he already knew all the right places on her body, knew when to keep it slow to build her to a frenzy, knew when to give it to her hard and send her flying. And knew when she needed him to do to her whatever he wanted.

"Oh, yes." Her makeup would be wrecked and her hair would be a mess, but a moment later she couldn't think of anything except him inside her as she clenched her teeth against the pleasure and dug her fingernails into his shoulders. Her legs went around his waist on some inclination all their own, locking at the ankles. She hadn't bothered to kick her heels off, needing to revel in how sexy and desirable she felt wrapped around him half-clothed. "Just like that."

"So sweet." He groaned, keeping his pace, his jaw pulled tense as his gaze burned at her like flame through emeralds. She lost her breath as the heat they produced together rose to a blistering fullness. "Are they?"

She knew what he meant, but at that precise moment, she couldn't answer him. She came like a slingshot had flung her toward the sun. Evan abandoned his slow pace to join her, his groans in her ear and the new strength of his thrusts powering her ascent. But she knew him well enough to realize she wouldn't be able to avoid his questions for long.

"They're for you," she whimpered as she descended from the heights, drifting between exhaustion and euphoria. Thank God, this was finally done. "You've given me back everything he took away, and then some."

The tension in his body flowed out of him, and he relaxed into her embrace. "I'll give you more than he ever did."

He would, she thought as he gathered her closer, putting his lips to her ear as she shivered. His hands prowled her tenderly, molding to each curve before moving to the next. She was already boneless, but when his lips slanted over hers again and again, she thought she was going to melt through the desk. But she needed her senses, had to sort all this out. "What happens now?"

He smiled, tracing a finger down her face. "Well, right now we'll compose ourselves for a few minutes, and then I'll take you to lunch. Then I'll go kick your boss's ass in court, since you've reenergized me. Tonight, I'll take you home, and I won't let you leave. You won't spend Christmas like you did last year. You'll spend it with me. I'll take you to Florence to meet my family there, if you want. Next summer I'll take you wherever you want to go. At some point during all this, I'll take you to the altar, if you'll have me — "

"I'd marry you in a heartbeat, Evan Ross." The words tumbled out in an emotional tangle of laughter and indescribable relief. She'd seen him at his best and at his worst through the years. Whether he was ecstatically happy, fighting mad, sick or down in the dumps, she'd loved him all the same. "I've known you long enough to be certain of that."

He quickly put his finger to her lips. "Not another word. I refuse to tell our kids I proposed to you on my office desk."

"Why not?" she joked. "They can know Mom and Dad were so in love they had to maul each other wherever the mood struck."

He laughed. "True. But give me time to do this right. To

give you everything you deserve. And I will, I promise."

"Oh my *God*," she whimpered. "Just tell me this isn't a dream."

"It's real. And speaking of dreams, I want you to follow yours. Don't you dare let me keep you from it."

Her lips curled. "So you're gonna make me go to law school?"

She could let that smile of his eat her alive and she'd die happy. "Yep. It's a requirement." He laughed as she pinched him on the side. "I mean it, if you want to go to law school, then go, and I will support you all the way. I'll even throw in free tutoring. Wait until you see *my* Socratic method, baby."

Her burst of laughter agitated more tears, sending them trickling over her cheeks. He reached up to wipe them away. "And from now on I'll make sure this is something you'll do only out of joy, and never pain."

They strolled from his office twenty minutes later with every semblance of professionalism. Kelsey had reapplied her lipstick and managed to tame her hair, but she knew nothing would remove the sensuous satiation from her face. Evan didn't hesitate to hold her hand as they walked down the hall, giving her the sense that it was them against the world.

Delilah looked up from her computer as they passed, her expression freezing when she spied them. Kelsey gave her an obnoxious smile and a shrug as they went by. She could swear she heard the other girl snatch up her phone and start dialing before she and Evan could get out the door.

Outside, the rain had stopped and a sliver of blue struggled to break through the overcast, but the world still glistened with remnant raindrops. Evan held open the door of his sleek black truck for her and she climbed in, so grateful to be back there again. Back in his life the way she wanted to be. Her gaze never left him as he walked around to get in the driver's side, utterly delectable in his dark gray suit. Hers, finally. For once, she considered herself the luckiest girl on earth.

"I have one question," she said as he settled himself in the seat and brought the engine to life. "Did you really keep this trip after you and Courtney split up because you wanted to take me? It won't hurt my feelings if you say no."

He grinned. "After it all blew over, and I remembered I needed to do something about this trip, you're the first person who came to mind. You usually are. Think about it, when you called me that day last Christmas to tell me about Todd and Courtney, don't you remember what I asked you?"

"I don't remember much. You didn't say anything for so long I thought you'd hung up."

"Yeah, but then…?"

The memory unfurled, smoothed out like a crinkled-up piece of paper. Kelsey's lips curled upward.

Evan! Oh, God, get over here. Get her out of my house.
What? Who?

Todd and Courtney are sleeping together! I just caught them in my bed! Come get this whore out of my house!

The dead silence on his end was usually as far as she let her memory get, because the thought of her hysterical screech was enough to mortify her until her dying day. If she'd let it play out…

Kelsey, are you all right?
No! Evan—

Just stay away from them until I get there, do you hear me? I'll be there in ten minutes. I'll kill that son of a bitch for doing this to you.

She nodded. "I remember." He'd always seemed far angrier over Todd hurting her than any wrong done to himself.

"He really did me a favor, and I knew it. But you were hurt, and you needed time to get over it. I wanted to make sure you were. You scared me, though." He trailed a finger down her cheek, the gesture full of meaning.

Kelsey scoffed. "If you had told me how you felt all those years ago, I never would have left that party with him. I'd have stayed with you."

"I know that now, and yes, I feel like that much more of a dumbass because of it."

"Don't. No more of that. Let's just look ahead." But they *could* talk about it now, she realized. She could think of her college days and the Todd-and-Courtney fiasco without the slow burn of fury slithering through her, or feeling like she wanted to hit something. Or just shutting down completely. Finally, the wall between her and Evan was broken down, and in its place was a connection she never could have imagined.

"Sounds good." He reached across to link his fingers through hers, never letting go as he navigated the damp streets.

A new thought struck her as he pulled into a parking space at their favorite restaurant. "One more thing, though. You never did read everything I wrote about you."

He put the truck in Park, smiled and leaned over to kiss her. "I don't have to. Every time I look at you now, I can see it all."

Epilogue

Evan didn't think he'd ever seen Kelsey look more beautiful than on their wedding day. He stood on the beach with Brian at his side and watched her slow approach, a dream in white with the morning Hawaiian sun glowing on her sundress. If his jaw was clenched in desire and his hands were shaking with the need to get her out of that dress, no one noticed—except maybe her—because all eyes were on her, and hers on him.

She'd agonized over wearing a white dress. "Evan," she'd despaired, "it seems a little ridiculous to wear white since I've already been married once and now I'm knocked up. I mean, come on."

"But only one other person knows about that last part," he'd told her, grazing a knuckle over the little bulge of her belly. The fact that his baby was growing in there made him happier than anything in his entire life ever had.

"I saw your mom looking at me funny, Evan. She was looking at my boobs."

And he'd cleared his throat and stuttered that it was kind of hard *not* to. Which had made her sock him.

They were keeping Kelsey's pregnancy quiet until after the wedding, not out of shame or any desire to fool anyone — though it was quite possible Kelsey's mother would faint dead away when she found out — but because they didn't want all the focus to be on that detail today. They had six more months to celebrate their impending arrival. Today was for them.

If any of the guests had been looking closely, they might have noticed that when the wind blew just right, Kelsey's flowing dress rippled back and molded to the slight swell of her stomach. She held her bouquet of calla lilies down low trying to conceal it. God, she was so lovely she made his chest ache, her spiraled hair gathered softly at the nape of her neck, the sun glistening on her tanned shoulders. A pink lei hung around her slender throat. It was a struggle for Evan to swallow around the dryness in his mouth.

He'd worn solid white, too, to appease her, and because she'd told him it looked unbelievably sexy on him. He didn't know so much about that, but whatever made her happy.

And thank God he'd talked Brian into dying the damn blue streak out of his hair, just for this one event. Though his brother vowed that in return he was going to dye every strand of it blue. Or red or purple, he hadn't decided yet. Maybe a Mohawk. He'd brought Michelle to Hawaii with him, and she looked astoundingly normal. She was also madly in love with Brian. Poor girl. But at least he was working hard on opening his own tattoo parlor.

Lisa, proud matron of honor and the sole bearer of their secret, was practically bouncing in her spot as Evan shook hands with Kelsey's father and drew his bride up beside him for their vows. Kelsey's fingers were trembling and he gave them a reassuring squeeze. She wasn't crying yet. She didn't cry until they were pronounced husband and wife. And then he didn't have to wait to be told to kiss his bride. She threw her arms around him and kissed her groom amidst cheers and whoops and applause. And kissed him and kissed him. Lisa threatened to grab Kelsey's lei to drag her off.

When Evan led her back up the aisle of seats set up on the beach, he leaned close to her ear and whispered, "How are you feeling?"

"I didn't blow chunks during the ceremony, so we're good," she hissed back through her smile. They laughed and the photographer snapped a picture—*that* was going to be a good one. No one would ever know they'd been smiling and laughing at one another while whispering about the possibility of her throwing up during the wedding. It might not seem the smartest thing, scheduling it for the morning given her condition, but hell—she was afflicted with morning sickness, noon sickness, night sickness…so any time they picked would've been a crapshoot. And he hadn't liked the thought of her suffering out here through the worst of the day's heat.

They held a brunch at the resort for their families and friends who had flown out, during which they entertained them by smearing cake all over one another and generally being incapable of keeping their hands off each other. Evan was careful not to agitate Kelsey's equilibrium during their first dance as a married couple.

Brian managed to get through a surprisingly eloquent toast without calling Evan an assortment of epithets even once. Lisa dropped no less than two-dozen hints about the baby in her own toast, which was about the beauty of friendship blossoming into love. Kelsey only had to run and throw up once. By then the mimosas were flowing and no one even noticed her flee, but to Evan it was an effective end to the festivities. He had a wife now, and he needed to take care of her.

Lisa ducked into the ladies' room to get Kelsey washed up and presentable again while Evan waited in the hallway, and by the time they emerged she looked just as fresh and lovely as she had on the beach.

"Sorry," she whispered to him, her expression pained. "It's the smell of the food. Even though I want to eat every bite of it."

"Yep," Lisa said, nodding in fond remembrance.

"Honey, *I'm* sorry you're having the day spoiled for you like this."

"Oh, no! It's not spoiled. Nothing could spoil today for me." She put her hand on her belly and smiled at him. "It's worth it."

Lisa erupted in tears and pulled them both in for a hug. "Oh my God, y'all are so *sweeeeet*!"

"Lisa," Kelsey wheezed around the shoulder in her throat. "I'm the hormonal one. I know with us it's usually the other way around."

"Oh, shut up." Lisa released them, wiping her streaming eyes. Evan handed her his handkerchief, which she took and dabbed at her cheeks. "I'm just so happy for you. You don't even know."

"Sure we do, I just hope I'm not going to bother you too much, calling you and asking about every little thing."

"I don't care if it's four in the morning, call me. After having three, I'm like the expert. And I'd better be one of the first ones you call when the time comes, too."

"You will be," Evan assured her. "Godparents are always high on the list."

Lisa only dissolved in tears again at that bit of news, burying her face in Evan's handkerchief, and it took several minutes of soothing for them to get her to stop the waterworks. "So when are you telling everyone else? Because I'm about to burst here," she asked when she was capable.

"That's obvious," Kelsey said dryly. "I wonder if there's anyone in the room who *doesn't* know by now, thanks to you. We're thinking right after we get back from the honeymoon, though. Can you last till then?"

"It'll be hard, but I think I can."

The view from their suite bedroom was spectacular, even better than the year before. Kelsey stood at the window, watching the crystal blue waves roll in on the beach where she and Evan had just stood becoming husband and wife. The sun caught on the whitecaps, turning the surf to diamonds. It sparkled almost as much as the one on her finger. The ring hadn't left her hand since Evan slipped it on there at Christmas in Florence, standing outside the Duomo.

She still couldn't believe it.

Absently stroking her hands over her belly, she heard him enter the room behind her and turned to smile at him. "It's even better than last year, I think."

But *he* was quite possibly the most beautiful sight she'd ever beheld, wearing white slacks and a loose white long-sleeved shirt buttoned up under his lei. His hair was still wind-tossed, and he raked a hand through it as he walked over to put his arms around her from behind, his hands joining hers on her stomach. "How are you feeling?"

Anticipation shivered through her. "Really good right now."

"Mmm. You feel really good to me, too."

She giggled and tilted her head as his lips trailed over the side of her neck. "I'm so happy. It was beautiful, don't you think? Perfect."

"It was. But all it needed was you there to be beautiful and perfect."

"Sweet talker." She turned into his embrace. "So what if someone had told you just before our first trip here that we would be back in a year, getting married, with a baby on the way?"

His lips grazed the tip of her nose. "I wouldn't have believed it, but I'd have thought, 'Damn, that would be incredible.'"

"Really? You don't wish we could have waited a bit?"

"Ten years, Kelsey. Don't you think we waited long enough?"

"Oh, I definitely think so."

Her law school dreams had been put on hold for a bit, but it was okay. As she'd told Evan when she first discovered she was pregnant, another dream of hers had always been to have a family, to be a mom. It didn't really matter to her which came first, but fate had decided for them. And though the baby was unplanned, he or she was definitely not unwanted by either of them.

Evan kissed her, his lips soft, his tongue gently exploring. She could swear every time he kissed her was like the first time, unleashing a flock of fluttering wings in her stomach. She tangled her fingers in his hair, reveling in this sweetness. Ever since Kelsey had told him about the baby, it seemed everything about him had gentled. The way he touched her, kissed her, looked at her, made love to her.

He drew her back to the bed and sat on the mattress. Smiling, she hiked her dress up to her thighs and straddled him, sinking back into his kiss once she had settled on his lap. His fingers skimmed her thighs, roamed up to brush her breasts. Slowly, carefully, he pulled her dress down while she drew away and bit her lip at the friction of the elastic rubbing over her too-sensitive nipples, even through her strapless bra. His fingers brushed her back as he made quick work of that as well.

"Oh, thank you," she murmured once that itchy aggravation was gone, replaced with his soothing caresses. She had to smile at how mindful he was of her tenderness there. His tongue gently laving her swollen flesh was like a warm balm. He didn't have to tell her that he enjoyed all the swells and curves pregnancy had blessed her with. He'd shown her almost every day, if only in the way he looked at her.

"Thank *you*," he said after a moment, and lifted his head to nuzzle against her neck.

"Evan, I love you so much."

"I love you. My wife." He smiled at her before taking the dress bunched around her midsection and lifting it over her head, leaving her in nothing but her lacy white panties.

My wife. Those words sang through her. She pulled off his lei and began working the buttons on his shirt, eager to bare all that smooth, hard male flesh to her feverish hands. The bottom button slipped loose and she gave his cock a long, languid stroke through his pants that made him hiss in a breath. He shrugged his shirt off his shoulders and she stripped it the rest of the way.

She couldn't be bothered with disrobing further. She freed him from his pants and he tugged her panties to the side, his urgency tempered with trembling care as she lifted her hips and sank onto his straining length. "Honey—"

"I want you. Now. I won't break," she whispered, bearing down to take more of him and nipping at his ear.

"I know, but oh, God, I might."

She started to laugh, but it turned into a moan when he moved his hips beneath her and her need ran rampant, bringing every nerve ending to sizzling life. It was always this way with him. Her bones evaporated and her muscles melted into him until he was all that was holding her up. "Evan, I…"

He slid his hands under her rear and shifted so that she was on her back and he was braced above her. Much better for the times when he turned her into melted butter. And this, their first joining as husband and wife, had effectively done just that.

Later, as they lay naked and exhausted across the bed, Evan's hand spread across the swell of her stomach. She loved how he did that, a sweetly protective gesture. They fell asleep like that every night, and usually in the morning she opened her eyes to feel him caressing her there. Like he couldn't keep his hands away from her. "Gorgeous," he murmured.

She chuckled. "Think you'll say that in five months or so? When I waddle like a duck and you have to tie my shoes for me?"

"I'll say it then and forever. I can't wait to see you in five months. You'll be even more beautiful. I never realized what a miracle it is."

It was, indeed, a miracle. Like them getting a second chance at doing things right. She wouldn't waste time thinking about the four years she'd spent married to the wrong man. Those years only made her all the more appreciative toward the one who loved her now. Made her thank God for him. Things truly happened for a reason.

"Hey," he said suddenly, just as she was about to drift off. "Now that we're married, I have something to tell you. It's been bothering me for a long time. It's time I got it off my chest."

Ordinarily, after what she'd been through, a statement like that would have sent her into a panic. Not now, not with him. She was curious, but not frantic with worry, riffling through a dozen mental images of him betraying her in some way. She had that much trust in him. "Oh?"

"Remember that first night at my house last year? When you got drunk?"

"How could I forget?"

"Did you by any chance have a really hot dream?"

Keep reading to enjoy *Barely Leashed*, a bonus short prequel!

Bonus Material

BARELY LEASHED — A SHORT PREQUEL

Christmas sucks.

No, that wasn't true. She loved Christmas. Christmas *parties* sucked.

"We're not staying long," Todd grumbled, steering the truck carefully into the circular driveway of the palatial Ross home. Kelsey Jacobs looked at her husband's profile — downturned mouth, brows set low, muscles hard around his eyes — and sighed.

Actually, no, Christmas parties didn't suck, either. She loved the entire season: the lights, the festivities adding warmth despite the chilled air, the music.

Having a husband with some kind of perpetual case of male PMS, now that drained the enjoyment right out of everything.

Everything. She couldn't let his bah-humbug attitude rub off on her anymore. It was pulling the life out of her.

She let her gaze roam over the spectacular, brightly lit

house and felt a little thrill to hurry and get in there. The place always took her breath away, but even more so when every line of it was precisely defined with a string of tasteful clear Christmas lights. She should've told Todd to stay at home, but that wouldn't have worked. She couldn't walk in there alone, couldn't face the questions. Todd wouldn't have gone for that, anyway.

Always keep up appearances, her mother often said. But her mom had never had to deal with this.

"We don't have to stay long. We never do," she muttered. "But can you please get through the night without snapping my head off?"

Or completely ignoring me in front of everyone? she finished silently when he failed to reply. Though sometimes his silence was preferable over any words he might have for her.

"I'm just tired," he grumbled after several seconds passed.

"Okay. I'm tired too." *So get over it.* "But you know we'd never hear the end of it from Evan if we didn't show up."

"Evan seems to forget that we never drag him to stupid crap against his will."

Once again, she got the eerie sensation that Todd was *trying* to pick a fight. It was the only explanation for some of the off-the-wall things he said lately. Lashing out at Evan, his best friend since childhood, hers since college? What had Evan done to deserve that? The thing was, it wasn't the first time Todd had done it, and it was getting worse.

"Are you mad at Evan for some reason you haven't told me about?"

She practically sensed Todd stiffening in the driver's seat. "No."

Maybe he's mad at him for introducing the two of us in the first place.

The thought occurred so easily to her because lately there

were times she felt the same way toward their matchmaker. But that wasn't fair, was it? Evan had only introduced them. He'd never encouraged them to hook up; in fact, she didn't think he'd been too happy about it. Maybe that should've been a red flag to her.

As soon as they entered the foyer and the swirl of color and activity inside the house, the masks of a happy couple went into place. Todd even made a show of helping her slip her coat off her shoulders, so she did her part and linked her arm through his as they accepted greetings from friends and acquaintances.

Smiling, laughing, warmly thanking those who complimented her silky green dress, she let not one iota of melancholy infiltrate the façade. It wasn't too difficult, what with the festive atmosphere. The towering Christmas tree alone could melt the coldest heart, glistening with lights and ornaments she'd be afraid to touch, let alone allow to dangle several feet above the ground. Holiday tunes drifted languidly over the merry chatter.

Through the crowd, she saw Evan standing in a circle of people with his arm loosely around his fiancée's waist. That familiar little thrill zinged through Kelsey's chest. She couldn't fight it, so she didn't even try. She could only let it wreak its havoc on her heart; she could torture herself about it later.

Evan hadn't only been her best friend through her last two years of college, but she'd been so infatuated with him it was a miracle she'd kept her wits about her enough to hang around him without making a fool of herself. To him, she'd been like a kid sister. His favorite kid sister, but still. It hadn't been nearly enough for her.

The years since had dampened the agony somewhat, but that little twinge she felt every time she laid eyes on him had never gone away.

Courtney, his fiancée, looked beautiful as usual, her hair

twisted up into a soft mass of gold with loose ringlets brushing her naked shoulders. Her burgundy dress allowed for a lot of bare skin and her usual eye-popping cleavage. Evan would probably relish sliding that clinging bodice down later, replacing it with his lips and...

Kelsey felt her own lips twist and would have torn her gaze away before such thoughts could take hold. Inevitably, it always led to her imagining herself in Courtney's place, and shame was always right on the heels of those fantasies. How would she feel if she knew Todd was having such thoughts about another woman? Horrible, that's what.

Yeah, and maybe if Todd had laid a hand on you in the past three months...

As Courtney lifted a champagne glass to her full red lips, her engagement ring sparkled.

Kelsey stared at it, mesmerized, feeling her mouth run dry with...what? Jealousy? That was ridiculous. Evan was her friend above all else, and he deserved to be happy. Kelsey even liked Courtney somewhat, though she didn't see what differentiated her so much from the usual parade of gorgeous arm candy she'd seen at Evan's side over the years. What was it about *her* that had earned her that sparkler when so many others before her had tried and failed to obtain it?

She felt Todd's arm pull away, startling her out of those useless thoughts. Without that anchor, she was set adrift in misery again. He was talking to someone now, and after a moment, walked away without a word to her. Not that she needed him at her side every moment, but these were mostly his friends, not hers, with only a few exceptions. She could party and have fun with the best of them, but she wasn't good with a roomful of mostly strangers. The four years she'd lived here, far from her native Mississippi, hadn't been spent socializing.

Kelsey glanced at Evan to see him looking back at her, his

expression grave. Then his lips curved in a smile and motioned her over with the slightest tilt of his head.

Relieved, she took a step in that direction, only to be intercepted by her coworker, Lisa Scott. The one true friend she'd made since moving here.

"You're here! I'm so glad!" Kelsey exclaimed as Lisa gave her a quick hug. "You have *no* idea."

Lisa laughed, and they spent the requisite five minutes cooing over each other's dresses and shoes and hair. Lisa looked positively radiant, but then with her enormous blue eyes, chiseled features and shimmering blond hair, she always did. Lately she'd had an undeniable glow about her.

Lisa lifted a glass of champagne from the tray of a server who was passing by and handed it over to Kelsey. "Here. You probably need this."

"Is it that obvious?"

"No, I mean…just drink. Yeah. Drink on that for a few minutes."

"Okaaay." Kelsey looked at her as if she'd lost her mind, but obliged. Lisa was probably right, anyway. If she was going to get through tonight, she needed some help. With the warmth of the champagne spreading through her chest, she felt a little better. It was really, *really* good, but then the Rosses spared no expense. "What is that you're drinking?"

"Me?" Lisa looked down at the glass she held as if she suddenly wanted to hide it behind her back. "Oh…um. Club soda."

Kelsey laughed. "You might need something stronger than that, yourself."

Lisa's smile faded. "Right. I kind of…have something to tell you. So drink some more."

Pregnant. She's pregnant again.

Eyes widening, Kelsey grabbed Lisa's arm. "Oh my G— Lisa, are you…?"

Sighing, Lisa nodded. "Yes. I just found out today. And before you say anything, I know. It wasn't planned, and I'm more than a little freaked out. But we're happy about it."

"Congratulations!" Kelsey leaned over to give her another hug. "You *should* be happy about it. No wonder you're glowing. I'm so thrilled for you."

"Really?" Lisa searched her face anxiously as they parted. "I was nervous, because… well, I know how badly you want to start trying to have one of your own. I didn't want your feelings to get hurt."

Kelsey fought down the little green-eyed monster that was indeed threatening to gnaw its way into her thoughts. Until earlier this year when their problems had really started, she'd been asking Todd when they could start trying to conceive. During those conversations, he'd always suddenly found something far more interesting on TV or in the newspaper. Finally, she'd quit talking about it, hoping he might bring it up someday. That day had never come.

She waved her hand dismissively at Lisa's comment. "Don't worry about that. I'm sure we'll get there eventually. In the meantime, I'll just have my fun babysitting yours."

"And you know I'll be calling, girl. I need date nights to keep my sanity."

Kelsey laughed and gestured to Lisa's still-flat belly. "Are you sure date night isn't the cause of all this?"

"More like moments of utter, careless stupidity." Lisa fidgeted. "There's something else."

Kelsey's heart dropped. "You're quitting work." Hopefully she'd spent all of her powers of deduction on Lisa's first revelation. She didn't want to think of going to that office without her. *No, no, no.* But there was no rush of denial from her friend, so she knew she'd been dead on again.

"Drew is only six months old, and Kayleigh doesn't start school for another year. I just can't do the whole working mom bit anymore. I don't want to. Plus we'll be spending so much on day care, it's ridiculous. I plan on giving two weeks' notice next Friday. I'll be gone by the first of the year."

"Well, I understand. But you have no idea how much I'll miss you."

"Hey, I'll still be around. We'll do lunch as often as we can."

"Deal."

This night really freaking sucks.

Smiling to cover the deepening of her melancholic mood, Kelsey glanced around the room. The first time she'd stepped foot in the Ross home, years ago, she'd done nothing but stare and gape and marvel. And not just at Evan. At that point, she'd been busily trying to stomp out the last smoldering embers of her raging inferno of a crush on him. She'd been committed to building a relationship with Todd, having accepted that Evan was never going to want her. Not the way she wanted him to.

She tried now to never revisit those memories, but it was hard, especially at times like this. Times when she knew her husband wasn't happy, she wasn't happy, and she didn't know how to fix it.

Suggestions of a long vacation with just the two of them had been promptly slapped aside. Subtle hints that maybe they should seek marital counseling had earned little more than cold stares. A few times, she'd asked outright what she could do to make things better. Silence had usually been the answer. Or a sigh. Or a terse "We're fine, Kelsey."

So, she'd given up. Probably not the smartest thing to do, but she couldn't fix a marriage by herself, and that's how Todd made her feel sometimes. Like she was in this alone.

It wasn't supposed to be this way.

The crowd shifted and she caught another glimpse of Evan standing with Courtney, laughing at something someone was saying. Somehow they looked even more stunning together than they had moments ago, his dark good looks contrasting with her blond beauty in a truly eyedazzling display. *They'll make beautiful babies*, she thought miserably, and immediately chided herself. Of *course* Evan had the most beautiful girl in the room on his arm. Of course that girl loved him. It only stood to reason. As the most gorgeous man she'd ever laid eyes on—no use denying it—and one of the nicest, he deserved no less.

But she also couldn't deny there were times she looked at Courtney and wished to God that whatever he saw in her, he could've somehow seen in Kelsey ten years ago. Then maybe she wouldn't be where she was right now.

How wretchedly selfish.

Lisa was following her gaze, and she should have known better than to get anything by her. "Oh," she said. "Kel, I'm sorry."

Kelsey blinked and looked at her friend, frowning. "For what?"

"Well…never mind. I need to shut up."

"What, Lisa? It's okay to say it."

"It's just that I know how you always felt about him, and now he's getting married, and you're having such a tough time… And I had to go and drop my bombshell. It must be hard, that's all."

"Really, Todd and I are…"

Fine. We're fine, dammit. How many times can you tell that lie without breaking down?

If she didn't watch it, she was going to find out. There was an uncomfortable stinging sensation behind her eyes even now.

She cleared her throat. "We're fine. Every marriage has its ups and downs, doesn't it? I guess you could say we're fully entrenched in a 'down' right now, but it'll be okay. It has to be."

Lisa didn't look convinced, her brows drawn together and her blue eyes troubled. Kelsey put her lips to her fluted champagne glass and shot another glance in Evan's direction. He was standing behind Courtney now with his arms around her waist, talking to his younger brother, Brian—well, arguing with him was more like it. She had to smile. Brian definitely marched to the beat of his own drum. He wore a long black sweater and baggy burgundy leather pants. His black hair sported festive red and green streaks, and underneath the arms of his sweater, she knew he had full tattoo sleeves. He drove Evan nuts sometimes, and no two brothers had ever been more different.

She wanted to go talk to them, hang out, have a good time like a true best friend should be able to. But tonight she didn't know if she could face it. Todd had been right to want to leave early, after all.

Speaking of…

Daniel came to sweep Lisa off to dance, and Kelsey scanned the room for her own husband. They could at least *attempt* to put up a pretense of happiness. How telling was it for them to come to a party and spend the entire night on opposite sides of the room?

As she moved across the floor, she was intercepted a few times, every single person asking if Todd was there, how he was doing…driving home the reality that all of these people were *his* friends first, except for Evan. He was the only person in this house besides Lisa she could honestly say was her friend, too.

He could never know how grateful she was to have him, one of the few constants in her life when she'd moved to a strange town straight out of college to start a new life. She often thought she'd leaned on him throughout that time as much as she had Todd. If not more. He'd

always, always been there for her.

Feeling conspicuous, she stopped and scanned the room from her new vantage point near the shining beacon that was the Christmas tree, still not seeing Todd anywhere through the mingling crowd. Now she couldn't see Evan, either. Sighing, she sipped her champagne and glanced around for a casual acquaintance to chat with, so she wouldn't look like a stranded wallflower.

"Merry Christmas," a deep male voice murmured near her ear. Gasping, she turned to find Evan standing directly behind her, grinning like a fiend and dangling a little sprig of mistletoe above her head.

"Oh, you," she laughed, a hand fluttering to her chest as her heart skipped a beat and began pounding frantically. "Merry Christmas."

He leaned forward and she offered her cheek for the touch of his lips...when what she wanted, shamefully, was to feel the warm, full press of them on her own. It was wrong, but what was she supposed to do? She'd never managed to stomp out those last embers, and despite all her efforts, they would always smolder for him. She'd tried, oh, God, how she'd tried...

He laughed and hugged her after the chaste peck on her cheek, squeezing her tight. He always gave the best hugs, and they always ended too soon. "You look gorgeous, Kel."

"You're too sweet." Kelsey rarely complimented his looks because if she ever got started, she wouldn't be able to stop. His black silk shirt was the same color as his hair, his holly green tie brought out the similar hue of his irises. How many times had she stared into those eyes in college, during late night cramming or general bitching/commiserating sessions, and wondered what he would do if she grabbed him and ravished him?

Long gone were those days, and she could kick herself now for not taking a shot at it. Just one shot, and maybe things could have been different. But far more frightening than the thought of his rejection had been the thought of damaging what they already had: the most precious friendship she'd ever known. So she'd kept quiet. And suffered.

She had more important things to worry about at the moment, anyway. His scrutiny was sending a spreading warmth up her cheeks, and she cursed her ability to blush redder than the brightest Christmas ornament in a nanosecond. He'd always held that power over her, and he'd have to be blind not to see it. The humiliation of it burned hotter than anything else. Well, almost anything.

"Are you okay?" he asked.

"I'm fine," she said brightly. "I haven't seen your parents yet, but just in case I don't,

please tell them I said everything looks beautiful."

His narrowed eyes showed her he wasn't fooled for a minute. As long as she'd known him, he'd had a finely tuned BS detector, and put it shamelessly to use wherever she was concerned. Then again, he was a prosecutor. It was part of his job.

"Give me some credit, here," he said, giving her one of those piercing appraisals she felt all the way to her toes. The look that made defense lawyers tremble. She knew because she worked for one.

"Lisa just told me some news that…has me a little upset," she said, grasping for something, anything, to keep from blurting out the truth that underlay everything. *I'm miserable, Evan, utterly freaking miserable. At least some of it is your fault.*

"Is everything all right?"

"For them, yeah, it's great. It's actually wonderful news. I'm just feeling selfish and sorry for myself. Don't mind me."

"Well, it's easy to get bogged down in that stuff this time of year. But I won't allow you to be bummed out at my parents' party, not if I can help it. Come on, dance with me."

"Oh, Evan, no—"

Green eyes twinkling bright as the lights in the Christmas tree, he took the champagne glass from her hand and set it on a nearby table, then cut off her protests by grabbing her hand and dragging her toward the couples swaying to "I'll Be Home for Christmas". By the time they reached them, she was laughing too, enjoying the feel of his warm hand wrapped firmly around hers in a grip she knew better than to try to break. He took position and pulled her to him, the firmness of his body against hers and the gentle press of his hand at her waist taking her breath away.

They'd danced together before a handful of times, and the only time she hadn't gone soft as butter in his arms was at her wedding. He'd been Todd's best man. She'd been so happy, so eager to start a life with the man who'd managed to win her heart away, even if a tiny shard had always remained in Evan's possession.

"You can tell that friend of mine he's a damn fool to let you stand abandoned in the corner like that," he said. His tone was light, but she sensed anger behind the words. It drew her brows up in surprise.

"I think he's just—"

"I don't care what he's doing. I haven't seen him by your side since the moment you walked in."

"Well, where's Courtney right now?" she asked with a wink.

"Courtney's off doing Courtney's thing. She's my social butterfly. I don't have to worry about her."

"So...I'm *not* one, and you have to worry about me?"

"You're my shy violet and I always worry about you, whether you need me to or not. Do you want me to talk to him?"

"No," she snapped, much too quickly. "Please don't get

involved; you know how he is. That'll just make things worse."
Immediately, she winced at her slip.

And he, naturally, didn't miss it. A frown creased his brow.
"Are you two all right?"

Oh, God, don't even ask me that, you of all people will see the truth no matter what I say.

"Can I plead the Fifth?" she asked with a dull laugh. She feared her palm was about to grow damp in the heat of his, and she forced the fingers of her other hand not to tense on his shoulder. She shouldn't be having this conversation, not with him.

"Shit. Kelsey, I'm sorry."

At the despair in his voice, she shook her head vehemently, unable to bear another person she cared about apologizing for how much her life sucked. It could be far, far worse, couldn't it?

It wasn't like Todd was abusive, or cheating on her…

But in his coldness, in his neglect, he was tearing her to pieces. As for cheating…well, there were no mysterious business trips, no unexplained late nights, no walking in on secretive phone calls.

She had no reason to believe anything like that was going on.

"We'll be fine. Really, don't worry about us," she said.

"It's not him I'm worried about. You know, sometimes I wish I'd—"

He cut off, and her heart went wild as she searched his face for the end to that sentence.

"What?"

"Nothing. Never mind."

"Evan…"

He took that moment to separate them, giving her a little twirl as she nearly screamed in frustration. "I was about to say something utterly useless and unhelpful to the situation," he said, bringing her back close and settling his hand on the small of her back again. "Don't worry about it."

Sometimes I wish I'd never let you slip through my fingers? Sometimes I wish I'd grabbed you and run?

Yeah, right. Wishful thinking.

"Enough of my gloom and doom," she said, desperate to take the heat off herself. "Have the wedding plans begun in earnest?"

He chuckled, but the darkness hadn't bled out of his eyes any more than it had bled out of her mood. "Yeah. You can imagine."

"Is it still on for August, or can you two wait that long?"

"We *need* that long, if she wants to pull off something of this magnitude. Damn thing just keeps getting bigger and bigger. I've threatened elopement, if I have to drag her kicking and screaming."

"Just about every woman has dreamed of her wedding since she was a little girl. Courtney just wants it to be special."

"It'll be special all right. The kind of special that leaves us all bankrupt."

Laughing as he twirled her again, she found herself truly wishing Evan got everything he wanted out of life. No one deserved it more, at least in her eyes. She would suffer any hardship to know he was happy. There was comfort in the thought. "I hope she realizes what a lucky girl she is." *She'll get to wake up beside of you every morning for the rest of her life.*

"I hope she does, too," he said with a mock seriousness that made her laugh harder. Their dance turned into more of an affectionate hug, and she squeezed him tight, closing her eyes and breathing deep the mysterious spice of his cologne and the scent that was distinctly his. "And you keep your chin up," he said, his voice so near her ear that it sent a shiver down her spine.

"You're right, everything will be okay."

Her best friend. She might never have him the way she'd wanted all those years ago, but she was blessed to have him at all.

Opening her eyes just before he released her, she saw something curious over his shoulder. Just a brief glimpse of what appeared to be a couple arguing in the corner, which ordinarily wouldn't have been strange at a party. What caught her attention and held it so steadfastly for a brief moment was that the two people were Todd and Courtney.

She was about to comment, wondering what those two could possibly have to fight about.

They hardly spoke to each other aside from friendly chit-chat whenever the four of them were together. But it was then that Evan's dad came through the room in a Santa Claus suit, doing his yearly shtick with a merry "*Ho ho ho!*" Cheerful chaos ensued. She got caught up in the laughter, the moment forgotten.

Two weeks later, she would remember that moment again in excruciating detail, and wonder how she could have been so blind.

Author's Note

Dear Reader,

It all started in 2008 with a publisher's call for red-hot summer romance. The idea for *Unleashed* was born, but little did I know it would develop into a family saga, wherein all three of the Ross siblings and their closest friends find their happy-ever-afters.

I can't thank you, the readers, enough for making it all possible. Thanks to you and the many people in my team who have believed in this series over the years, the book you've just finished has had three lives: first with Samhain Publishing, then a stint as a self-published title, and now with the wonderful folks at Entangled. I couldn't be more grateful to be given this opportunity to bring you all of the Rosses in bright, shiny new packages. I hope you enjoy reading them (or re-reading them!) as much as I have enjoyed writing them.

I'd also like to give special thanks to the team at Entangled, to my agent, Louise Fury, and to Linda Ingmanson, who gave this story its very first chance at Samhain. I'm forever thankful and humble to have such amazing support, and such fabulous readers.

Never stop rockin'!
Cherrie

About the Author

New York Times and USA TODAY bestselling author Cherrie Lynn has been a CPS caseworker and a juvenile probation officer, but now that she has come to her senses, she writes contemporary and paranormal romance on the steamy side. It's *much* more fun. She's also an unabashed rock music enthusiast, and loves letting her passion for romance and metal collide on the page.

When she's not writing, you can find her reading, listening to music or playing with her favorite gadget of the moment. She's also fond of hitting the road with her husband to catch their favorite bands live.

Cherrie lives in East Texas with her husband and two kids, all of whom are the source of much merriment, mischief and mayhem. You can visit her at http://www.cherrielynn.com or at the various social networking sites. She loves hearing from readers!

Enjoy the rest of the Ross Siblings Series...

UNLEASHED

ROCK ME

BREATHE ME IN

LEAVE ME BREATHLESS

LIGHT ME UP

TAKE ME ON

WATCH ME FALL

Also by Cherrie Lynn...

SWEET DISGRACE

FAR FROM HEAVEN

RAW DEAL
Larson Brothers

RAW NEED
Larson Brothers

RAW HEAT
Larson Brothers

SHAMELESS

Discover more Entangled Select Contemporary titles...

How to Fall
a novel by Rebecca Brooks

Julia Evans puts everyone else first—but all that is about to change, starting with a spontaneous trip to Brazil. Now Julia can be anyone she wants. Like someone who's willing to have a wickedly hot hook-up with the sexy Aussie at her hotel. Except, Blake Williams may not be what he seems. Julia and Blake will have to decide if they're jumping into the biggest adventure of all or playing it safe.

Knocked Out by Love
a *Love to the Extreme* novel by Abby Niles

Brody "The Iron" Minton has been in love with Scarlett for as long as he can remember, but she's his best friend's ex, and only an ass would make a move. Except Scarlett wants help getting back in the dating game, and Brody's torn. If he helps her out, he can keep an eye on her and guard her vulnerable heart. But having the woman he's longed for for years in arms' reach is hell on a man's restraint. And the more time Brody and Scarlett spend together, the less innocent and safe the flirting and fun becomes.

28080537R00141

Made in the USA
Lexington, KY
09 January 2019